TO KATHARRINE

Urumqi

The Legend of Kanoka

ITS BEEN AWESOME BRING YOUR NEIGHBOR! DON'T FORGET TO KEEP IT REAL!

Nick Kostka

~ NICK KOSTKA

Copyright © 2008 by Nick Kostka

All rights reserved. No part of this book shall be reproduced or transmitted in any form or by any means, electronic, mechanical, magnetic, photographic including photocopying, recording or by any information storage and retrieval system, without prior written permission of the publisher. No patent liability is assumed with respect to the use of the information contained herein. Although every precaution has been taken in the preparation of this book, the publisher and author assume no responsibility for errors or omissions. Neither is any liability assumed for damages resulting from the use of the information contained herein.

This is a work of fiction. Names, characters, places, and incidents either are the product of the author's imagination or are used fictitiously. Any resemblance to actual events or locales or persons, living or dead, is entirely coincidental.

ISBN 0-7414-4519-0

Cover Design by Steve Kostka.

Published by:

INFINITY
PUBLISHING.COM
1094 New DeHaven Street, Suite 100
West Conshohocken, PA 19428-2713
Info@buybooksontheweb.com
www.buybooksontheweb.com
Toll-free (877) BUY BOOK
Local Phone (610) 941-9999
Fax (610) 941-9959

Printed in the United States of America

Printed on Recycled Paper

Published February 2008

Contents

Part One—People of the Land

1	The Legend of Ben Kanoka	1
2	Five Friends	4
3	Long Expected Party	9
4	Bad News on the Doorstep	12
5	The Evil of the Empire	16
6	'Are you Urumqi?'	19
7	Seven- Five Groups, Five Newcomers	23
8	A Difference of Opinion	28
9	A Different Urumqi; A Different Oro	31
10	Of Origins and Factions	35
11	The Conspiracy	40
12	Walked Away	44
13	The Imperial Scheme	47

Part Two—The Storm

1	The Stories	49
2	The Blasters	54
3	The Power of Urumqi	57
4	The Battle in the Canyon	62
5	The Compromise	66
6	Schemes	70
7	The Lovebirds	74
8	The Coast	80
9	Minor Confrontations	86
10	Impending Fear	93
11	Major Confrontations	97
12	Stop!	104
13	An Unexpected Party	108

Part Three—The Mountains

1	The Legend Continues	111
2	Time to Regroup	114
3	The Councils	118
4	The Army	123
5	Caliphia	128
6	The Lehdeo	133
7	The Fall of the Counselor	136
8	The Plot	140
9	Of Parents and Grandparents	145
10	The Empire at War	150

Part Four—The Fall

1	The Urumqi Reunited	155
2	The Forming of a Plan	160
3	A Gathering	164
4	The Battle Begins	169
5	A Lost Cause	174
6	Of Elders and of Warriors	180
7	One Chance at Triumph	186
8	One Final Moment	193
9	And So It Was	197
10	The Ships	202

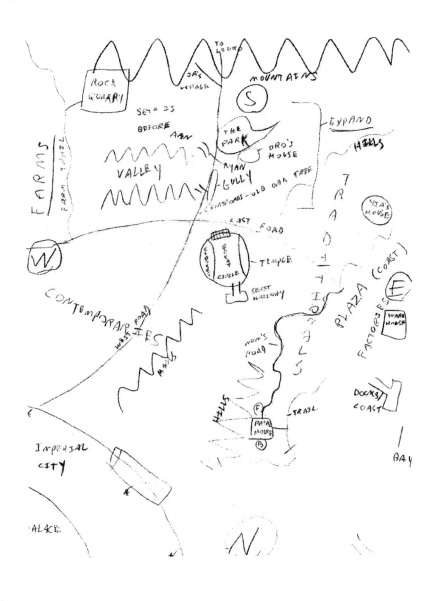

Part One- People of the Land

Chapter One- The Legend of Ben Kanoka

Urumqi. People of the land. The name meant something different to every person. Some said that they were the protectors of the good people who had lived as their neighbors. Others said they were mythical warriors who fought great battles against unknown evils that would otherwise plague the world. In a way, both of these descriptions are accurate, but not entirely. The unique role that the Urumqi played cannot be described by even the wisest of people.

You may wonder how I know so much about these ancient protectors. Well, in fact, I am the descendant of one of the greatest Urumqi who ever walked the mountains and valleys of Uru[1]. His name was Ben Kanoka. Those who know of the Urumqi usually know his name. The folk of Olde[2] say he was the greatest man who ever lived; not in any one aspect, but in a multitude of ways. Ben had never said a hateful word to anyone; had never hurt any other man's feelings; had never used others to benefit himself. This overwhelming benevolence on his part brought him many rewards. Some say that he only had one wish: he wished that everyone else's life could be as perfect and full of happiness as his own.

As in every great story of every great hero, I suppose there must always be a villain; an evil man who chooses not to see the light of day, but only moves to take from it. I believe it started with Ben's brother. The Kanoka family had grown small at the time of Ben's birth. He now had but one brother, for their parents had since passed from the lands of Uru. Tib Kanoka was never a figure of importance. The folk back then saw him as merely an imperfect shadow of his brother. If Tib was kind to someone, Ben was kinder. If Tib gave a compliment, Ben thought of a better one. As much as Ben wished for his brother to be happy, nothing ever changed. The people of Uru worshiped Ben, and Tib received nothing kinder than a cold stare. Things were about to get ugly.

One night, when the moon was hidden behind the Circle of Fire[3], a band of ships surrounded the world of Uru. The peaceful land was instantly in the midst of a great war. Not one living man was left untouched by the war. Consequently, there was no man to write the exact events. I can only venture to guess the exact details of that night…The legend says they came with fire, axes, and clubs. They burnt, chopped and clubbed everything in sight. Some folk of Olde say that they brought great sticks that had the power of lightening and instant death. They rounded up every family in Uru except for one. Ben and Tib held off the evil men for a very long time. It is said that they used no weapons; they simply used their minds. No one understood how, but they did.

They lived, alone and isolated, for some time. As time passed, Tib grew weary and his judgment became impaired. He talked of crazy things; he said he wanted more than anything to know why, why he must live such a horrible life. It was shortly after that that He came. No one knew who He was. He wore clothes as strong as metal, yet as soft as silk. Lightning cracked over his body when He spoke. He came to the Kanoka brothers' abode and approached Ben without the slightest effort. A look of horror crossed Ben's face when his eyes fell upon Him. At His side, Tib stood smirking. Ben stepped forward and pulled out a wooden stick. It was beautiful, with carven figures across the flat front surface and a small knot at the top. Ben raised the staff and struck Him. The crash emitted a horrible cracking noise and lightning shot outward. Ben attacked Him again and again. He stood there laughing as the lightning continued to crackle about his body. He suddenly swung out with his arm; the old frail figure of Ben Kanoka fell to a crumpled heap on the ground. Then he disappeared. Yes, that is what the folk believe. No one knows how or why, but he was gone.

It is said that Tib fled because of guilt. He had found his brother's weakness and betrayed him. As far as I know, he never was seen again after he fled. It is still a mystery to me how the Kanoka family is still in existence. Ben and Tib were the last two men to carry the family name.

The legend of Ben Kanoka was told to me by my father. At the time that I first heard the tale, it had little meaning to me. In the latter years of my life, my father told me another story; his story. The legend of the Urumqi which I tell you now is the true story of my father's life…

Chapter Two-
Five Friends

The game was called Kaalah. Forty wooden pieces rested on the nine by nine board, two rows of five on each side. Two of the four starting players were still in the game. The other two had lost, for their Commanders were surrounded. Seeing the gap between the line of mahogany soldiers, the ash General crossed the length of the board. "Beat you again, Aan," said the tall thin boy, removing his finger from the piece. "Man Ja, I had twice as many pieces and you still got me," grumbled Aan. The third boy spoke up. "He beat ya fair and square Aan," said Seth. "I still don't know how you saw that move. How are you all so good at this?" That voice came from Nom Patal.

There were five people in the room. My father was the first. His name was Oro Kanoka. The other four boys were Oro's long time friends. Aan Huila and Oro had been friends for as long as anyone could remember. Ja Kahn was more of a mystery. Oro didn't even know where he lived. He was tall and wiry with jet black hair; much different than Aan, who was short and a bit overweight. The jolliest of them all, Seth Andora, was a recent addition to the group. His rather large family used to live in another part of Uru. The smallest and quietest of the five boys was Nom. He came from a much larger family, where his voice was often not heard. He, however, always listened and tried hard not to ignore anyone.

Of course, these five boys were not the only children who lived in the vast lands of Uru. They knew many other students from their studies at the Temple. Most children began attending the Temple when they were about eight or nine. After six years at the Temple, the students whose families wished them to have a higher education traveled across Uru to the Great Temple, where occupations of great skill were shown to the learners. Oro was glad that he and his friends would soon be making the trip. For Oro was thirteen, as were his friends, and they had all decided to make the great journey together and learn from the masters at the Great Temple. Thirteen was a significant age. Those who believe in the ancient writings of the Urumqi are told that thirteen is the proper age to reveal the Urumqi history and to apply this knowledge to everyday life.

Oro had not yet been told of his true ancestry. He didn't even know of the legend of Ben. All that troubled Oro now was the minor inconvenience of traveling to the Great Temple. But for now, it was the last day that he would attend the Temple, and he joined his fellow students in celebrating the first milestone in their educations. "I don't have time to practice. I've had so much work…no time to do anything," muttered Oro. "Nonsense, everyone has time for games," joked Aan. Ja folded the board in two and proceeded to put away the pieces. "Better be goin'," exclaimed Seth, "cuz we wouldn't wanna be late for the last day!" The five boys got up slowly and left Oro's house. Time was not an issue in Uru. No one was ever accused of being late. Tardiness showed irresponsibility, and only responsible students attended the Temples.

The boys nearly ran today, for they had spent too much time playing. In between a breath, Ja called out "they've made a new version of Kaalah now, eh?" "Oh yeah, we're getting it from the coast tomorrow," answered Seth. Nom spoke up. "How do y'all know when these things come out?" he asked with a humorously puzzled expression. "It's called reading," said Aan. "You go to the coast, find the signs, and READ them," he said with a bit too much emphasis.

They reached the Temple and split off to go to their first set of classes. Nothing unexpected happened that morning. Everyone was as happy as Oro; the tension of learning would finally be lifted. During lunch, no one stood still. Every single student was rushing around, for no one wanted to leave the Temple without saying goodbye to all of their friends. Oro and Nom were doing just that. They made a huge circle around the outside of the Temple, stopping to talk to some of the people they knew. "Hey Ryan," called out Nom. "Hey Nom, what's new?" he responded. Ryan Ridder was probably the most serious person that Oro knew. It seemed like he always had work to do and never had time for fun. "Maybe this summer you can learn to lighten up," taunted Oro. "Oh yeah, well maybe the Great Temple will teach you some respect," shot back Ryan. In his commitment, Ryan was second only to Wanda Mardi, who claims that she never missed a day at the Temple and always brought home perfect scores.

The next person they stumbled upon was an old friend of Oro's. She was tall, with long blonde hair, and a very cute girl in Oro's opinion; they were just friends. Her name was Ava Bera. She ran up to the two boys, her best friend Mandi close behind her. Oro didn't know her too well. "Last day, last day," called out Ava. "Now you've got plenty of time, three months actually, to plan that drama party you keep talking about," replied Oro. They all burst out laughing.

I'm afraid I don't remember who else my father talked to on that last day. I recall that Aan was still with Wendy. She was supposedly his girlfriend, but no one really knew exactly what was going on. Oro talked to them awhile. There were others around, all in good spirits as well. Zach Johnson was his usual easy-going self, as were Max Toko and Dave Datsun, the two strangest people in the lands of Uru. They mostly laughed and joked about the party that Oro and Aan planned to throw. Oro was known for his streak of wildness at parties, which everyone had their own opinion as to why.

Although the last session dragged on forever, class was soon over, and the students made a mad rush for home. From the Temple, there were two main roads- East and West. Nom lived rather far from Oro and the others; he followed the East Road home. On the West Road, Seth was sprinting far ahead of Aan and Ja. Oro was somewhere in between. Even though they would see each other many times over the summer, they all stopped at Oro's for one last farewell. Seth's place was just up the road. Aan lived higher up in the hills, and like I already explained, no one was quite sure where Ja lived.

Oro had a nice family; a family quite like my own, in many ways. He was an only child, who never had the worries of a sibling like the rest of his friends. His mother worked as an accountant; his father oversaw a stone quarry. Oro's parents were not his only family. He had two grandmothers, one of which lived quite close to him. Her name was Yia Kanoka, for she was his father's mother. She had no other family besides Oro and his parents. She was always there for him when the times became especially rough.

Uru was not a beautiful kingdom, like it was in the days of Ben. For thousands of years, it had been an Empire. 'He' was the first of these dreaded emperors that ruled the land since the Dreadful Day[4]. It is possible that when Ben died, so did the hope of the people of Uru. No one resisted the fire, axes, and clubs; no one dared to rise up against the Empire. The real Urumqi were few, and they were weak and too small in numbers to take on their foes. The houses of Uru were small and dilapidated, built deep into the hillsides that covered the island. Oro was fortunate enough to have a decent house, probably the nicest of any of his friends. The Kanoka home rested on the top of the West Hill[5], which was actually quite close to the Temple. The West Hill was bordered by a narrow, grassy meadow, which was known as "the Park". The Park had been Oro's hangout for as long as he could remember.

"Mom, I'm home," called out Oro as he pushed open the squeaky front door. There was no answer. She often worked late, but never on a day as important as this. He walked into the kitchen and found a note. *Oro, I have to work late tonight, the boss says the numbers aren't adding up right ... Dad will be home soon. Enjoy your summer.* He tossed the note aside and went up to his room. He quickly set up his Kaalah pieces, and he was soon a hero, strategically sweeping the board of any opposition.

The first few days of summer were uneventful. Most of Oro's friends were at home celebrating with their families. Some were even planning what to bring on the great journey that was ever so far away in Oro's mind. Yia had come to congratulate him as soon as she could. Oro thought she seemed a bit sad. "Aw, Oro, you've come so far. Get out to the Park with your buddies. It's much too soon to be thinking about the journey you know." Oro smiled. "Don't worry. Who ever heard of stressing over a day of travel for three months?" It was Yia's turn to smile. "I'll tell ya who. Your father never had time for the moment. Always had to know the future he did…Live in the present, dear. It's the only way to enjoy what you've got." At the time, my father didn't really understand just what those words meant.

Chapter Three-
A Long Expected Party

"You know sometimes I cannot believe it!" spat Aan. "She gets all the attention. Just because she's come back home. She can't even do basic math! What kind of profession is art? This was supposed to be my moment. But NO! It's all about my sister now!" They sat in Oro's room with their invitation list in front of them. Oro scratched a few notes onto the paper. "What can I say? My mom wasn't even HOME to say 'good job' or 'you made it'." They both looked over the list one more time. Oro counted. "Twenty people...that's not bad." "If you think about it, that's a heck of a lot though," said Aan. "I still think we're forgetting someone," muttered Oro "Ooh that's right...Nom wanted to know if a buddy of his from another school could come," remembered Oro. "Well, who is he? Where's he from?" asked Aan a little too quickly. "His name's Mac Kalomo...he doesn't attend a Temple." Aan looked suddenly angry "...and you want to invite him to our GRADUATION party? ...you said no to Wendy's friend Shelly and now you want to invite some loser who doesn't go to school?" Oro wasn't surprised. The Huila family was known for their extreme views in the field of education. But then again, Aan's sister *was* an artist... "Look, Aan, it's not a big deal. Do it for Nom, alright?" He thought for a moment. "Okay."

As usual, Seth was the first one to arrive at the Park on the day of the party. Seth ran, he never walked, and he always made it a point to be first to any event that was labeled with a time. On the other hand, Ja always came late. No one knew why. Perhaps it had something to do with his family. Aan soon arrived with boxes of things he deemed necessary to have at a party. When Nom showed up, Aan was nowhere to be found. "Yo yo, Nom, what's hapnin," called out Oro. He saw Mac walking beside him. "What news from the West Side, stranger," called out Mac a bit too loudly. Oro could tell that he'd get along with Max and Dave just fine. "You must be Mac," said Oro. "Welcome to 'Da Park'…Nom, you show him a good time; I'll be back in a bit."

He noticed that a few other people were coming. Ryan and Zach, followed by Wanda and another boy that Oro didn't know, made their way into the Park. "Hey Oro, where's Aan off to?" called Ryan. "He's around here somewhere," replied Oro. "You know Slay?" asked Zach, acknowledging the rather large boy next to Wanda. Oro shook his head. "That's Slay Ander," exclaimed Zach "long time buddy of mine." "Sup," said Oro quickly. His eyes were on Ava. She had just come skipping into the party scene with two other girls.

"Long time no see, Ava," he called out. "Only been a week," she said a little too seriously. There was a quick burst of laughter. "Hey Mandi, how you been?" joked Oro. "And who might you be?" he asked, acknowledging the short, dark haired girl. Ava looked confused. "Oh, right…Oro, this is Jade," she said quickly. "Hi," she said shyly. "Welcome to the Park…c'mon I want you to meet some of my friends," said Oro in a quiet voice he didn't use too often. "Sure," she said. Oro noticed her warm smile. He glanced over at Ava, but she wasn't paying attention. She was looking at Slay. 'Yeah right,' thought Oro, 'I'm worrying too much.' As he and Jade started walking toward the others, Oro couldn't help but wonder.

"That crazy kid there, Jade, that's Seth," joked Oro. Seth was like Oro, in the way that he was always happy to meet someone new. He quickly came over and the three of them were soon laughing so much that Seth spilled his drink all over his shirt. Oro glanced over his shoulder once again; he saw Aan. He wondered why Aan only talked to the 'important' people, the people who mattered to *him*. Oro also noticed that Nom was quietly talking to Mac. He waved them over. Mac was on his third drink, even more hyper than when he had first arrived. As Ja came running over, the chaos was complete. Everyone was splashing their drinks around truly having a great time. Oro was thinking too much. Why was it that this party had two groups? Just because he and Aan had planned it together was no reason for anyone to take sides. *Who do we like better? Aan and Ryan or Oro and Seth?* That idea was just stupid. He then wondered if the others wondered why he was so quiet. Just then, Seth tossed a can at him; Oro caught it, popped the top, and splashed it all over the group. Kids like Ryan or Wanda didn't like people who got wild at parties. Maybe that was why they were with Aan. He didn't care; he was having fun...

Chapter Four-
Bad News on the Doorstep

It had been two days since the party. Things were still quite boring. That was all about to change. While Oro was out, an Imperial messenger came to the door. His parents were both at work, so Yia had come over to tend to things. She answered the door. "Hello; it is mandatory that all persons of this household read this document and obey all rules written therein. Failure to do so will be considered an offense to the new Emperor. Do you understand?" She said nothing, grabbed the paper out of the messenger's hands and closed the door. She spent several hours reading through the entire document. When Oro returned, she would need to have a serious talk with him. 'I've already put this off for two weeks,' she thought.

Oro came in the back door. He had just returned from the Park. "Anyone home?" he called out. "Yeah," answered Yia from the other room. Oro knew something was wrong before he even saw her. "What's up?" he asked. "Oro, we gotta talk," she said. "I left your parents a note...let's take a walk to my place, shall we?" As they walked down the road, Yia told Oro of the legend of Ben and the Dreadful Day. Oro was fascinated by the story. After she was through, he asked questions like 'Who was He?' and 'How can people use their minds to fight?' Once they had reached Yia's little home, she began to give Oro the answers. "I'll answer the second question first," she offered. "It is because Ben Kanoka was an Urumqi, as are you."

"A *what?*" asked Oro. "An Urumqi, a keeper of the peace, a warrior with no weapons; it is all the same," explained Yia. "How do I know? It is simple. The Kanoka family have been Urumqi for many, many years. It is customary for the young Kanoka boys and girls to learn of this identity when they reach the proper age. Your father flatly refused to be an Urumqi, or to tell you the truth, because of his fear of the Empire." Oro tried hard to take everything in. "Why does the Empire not like the Urumqi? Are there other families who are Urumqi?"

"Can you not guess from what I have told you how the Empire began? Before the Dreadful Day, there was no Empire. 'He' was the first Emperor. 'His' children have ruled Uru ever since. As for your second question...ah, yes, there are other families. But, so far, it has mattered not. The Urumqi are too few and too weak to take on the Empire." Oro didn't understand. "But if the Urumqi have special powers, why can they not be used to stop the Empire?"

"You are very smart, Oro. Let me show you in a different way. 'Urumqi' literally consists of the ancient words Uru and Qi. Uru means land and Qi means people. So Urumqi means 'people of the land'. When 'He' came, the folk of Olde gave them the name Guranqi. Guran means ruler and Qi is added because it represents people. Over the years, the 'Qi' that the two names have in common no longer means people; it means those with special power. The Emperor is a Guranqi; a Guranqi is like an evil Urumqi."

Everything that Yia had said made perfect sense to him. It was as if he somehow understood it all at once. "But if we cannot take on the Empire, what am I to do? How can I choose differently than dad did?" Yia was more than prepared for this question. "I'll start by pointing this out...when Ben Kanoka was struck down...the moment before he fell...he smiled. No one knew why. He didn't know. Tib didn't know. What the Guranqi believe is that Ben smiled for a reason. Ben knew something that He didn't. The Empire maintains the belief that Ben knew of 'other Urumqi' who would continue to be rebels and strive to overthrow the tyrannical government system. For this reason, He decided to kill Tib. After all, Tib *was* an Urumqi. Before this happened, Tib decided to flee and was never seen again. To this day, the Emperor lives in fear that the descendants of Tib Kanoka will one day overthrow the Empire and rule Uru as a peaceful Republic."

Oro was still confused. Yia knew, so she kept explaining. "Although I have no way of knowing if we are truly descendants of Tib, I do know that you are an Urumqi. It is now your responsibility to find others like yourself and to unite what is left of our order and eventually bring down the Empire." Oro did not believe this was possible. He wasn't even sure if he could *find* other Urumqi. "How am I to do this? Who will I find? How do you know we are not alone?" "There is not much more I can tell you. In time you will understand. There is, however, one more thing." She held up the document that was delivered earlier that day. "Emperor Vora has died. His son Viron is now Emperor." Oro wasn't quite sure why this was so important. Yia continued. "Emperor Viron is…obsessed with finding the Urumqi. He has decided that every child age thirteen will attend mandatory "schools" in a vain effort to find the latest generation of Urumqi and destroy them before they grow powerful."

He didn't understand. How was it possible that the will of one man could take away his summer, not to mention his hopes of becoming a professional, in a vain attempt to save himself? The Empire had just made another enemy. "How am I to go without getting caught?" She expressed a puzzled look, and then replaced it with a smile. "The reason we are feared by Viron is that we have powers beyond what is expected of us. We can accomplish tasks through thought that would take normal men years of hard work. Instead of thinking to fight, we fight by thinking. Aside from his mind, an Urumqi has but one weapon."

She got up and walked over to a small curio cabinet. With a click, the locked snapped open and she opened the door carefully. Inside was a staff. It was no ordinary walking stick; it had a twisted pattern, etched in from the bottom, which ended in a 'ball' at the top. She lifted it carefully from its hiding place and handed it to Oro. "This is an Urumqi's most powerful weapon. I made this one for your father when he was your age. I've had it ever since. I now give this to you. With your mind as your ally and your staff by your side, you will go to the school and you will unite the Urumqi. You will know of whom I speak." It was now dark outside; the sun had since set. In a very different tone, she said, "You better get going...your parents'll get worried." Oro gave her a hug and left.

As he lay awake in bed that night, he knew something had changed. He no longer had to speak to Yia; she just understood. It was different with his parents. Sure, they were disappointed to hear about the bad news, but they did not truly understand what was happening. His father was not an Urumqi. Maybe that was why things were different. He remembered the words of an old song that Yia once sang to him. *Well I just heard...the news today. It seems my life...is gonna change. I close my eyes...begin to pray. Then tears of joy...streamed down my face...* 'Why tears of joy?' he wondered. 'What was the next line?' He didn't have time to worry about that now. There were much more important things to think about.

Chapter Five-
The Evil of the Empire

It had been four days since the messenger brought the document to the Kanoka house. Oro had exactly one day left of his summer. He had not heard from anyone since the arrival of the bad news. He wondered if any of his friends were Urumqi. After reading the document several times, he understood that those who lived along the West Road would attend the same Temple that he had attended for years. Those along the East Road would go to another location. 'Maybe my father is wise to fear the Empire,' he thought. It wasn't fair that the Empire had the power to split up people forever just because of where they lived. 'It could be a long time before I see Nom.'

Oro walked down the dirt road. He walked alone. As he approached the Temple, he could sense the fear and confusion that now lingered in this once friendly place. Nobody seemed to know where to go or what to do. Neither did Oro. The Great Circle[6] had been destroyed. In its place was nothing but a sea of densely packed gravel. The entry was sealed off by a towering black wall with little gates that allowed the students to pass through. Oro joined the masses of students struggling to get through the small gates. When he finally made it up to a gate, an attendant handed him a schedule printed on parchment. She then asked him for his name and address. Once his information was recorded, she let him through the gate.

In the middle of the Great Circle, which was now quite densely populated, Oro glanced at his schedule. The room numbers were done the same way as always. He then glanced over at the 'Subject' column. There were only four things listed there: Mathematics, History, Language, and Technology. At that moment, an extremely loud bell sounded from atop the wall. The people around him began running to their classes. A large, dark-skinned boy with long hair approached Oro. "This...is...where?" uttered the boy in very broken English. He was pointing to a room number on his schedule. "That... place...is ...there," answered Oro, pointing to one of the hallways. As he walked to his first class, he thought about the people who had never been to school before.

While he was in the hallway, the loud bell clanged once again from atop the wall that now guarded the Great Circle. He then opened the classroom door, immediately followed by three other students. The four of them stood in the back of the room, not knowing what to do. The instructor was a large, beefy man with heavy bloodshot eyes. He walked over to the four students and eyed them suspiciously. "It's the first class of the first day. Why are y'all late?" No one spoke. Oro then said "I thought we had five minutes, like always." The instructor snatched the schedule out of Oro's hand. "Well, son, if you read your schedule like the other 26 students in this class, you'd know that only two minutes are given for passing. TWO, NOT FIVE! Do you understand, boy?"

Once Oro and the others were assigned their seats, the lesson began. "First things first; all of you must check your schedule right now. Look at the first row; the subject column must read 'mathematics' and the classroom column must read '702'. If anyone has any problems, come forward and tell me NOW." Two girls walked up to him. He grabbed their schedules and narrowed his eyes to read them. "See that number? It says 502, not 702. Y'all must go to 502 right away before I report you to the guards!" The girls said nothing and walked away.

The material was completely redundant to Oro. His boredom caused him to start looking at the other students. It was easy to see who had attended the Temple before; those students were also bored, and looking around just like Oro. As for the others, they were also easily categorized. Some wore overly fashionable clothes and had fancy hairstyles. Some were so laden with weapons[7] that it was hard to see what their clothes looked like. Yet others wore tattered clothes and spoke little English. 'They must be hill people,' thought Oro. He looked at the back of his schedule; he didn't want to be late again. Noticing the 20 minute break for lunch, he thought about who he should try to find first. 'Aan will probably try to find me...so I'll try to find Ja...'

His next two classes weren't much better than the first. History was a boring rehash of information he already knew. English was simply a nightmare. Apparently, the instructor didn't know that about a quarter of her students did not know how to speak proper English. Oro offered to help some of the people who were having trouble. Most of his offers were rejected, but he kept asking anyway. After awhile, he began to notice the people again, and there they were: the weapons, the fancy clothes, the hill people... He wondered why everyone seemed to be part of a group. Everyone, except him.

Chapter Six-
'Are you Urumqi?'

During his lunch break, Oro walked around the Great Circle keeping his eye out for Aan or Ja. After his second time around, he began to give up hope of finding anyone in this now dreadfully crowded courtyard. As he turned to find somewhere to sit, he noticed a hallway at the back of the Circle. At first, he didn't know why it caught his eye. He then noticed that very few people were coming or going. He went to investigate. Six years at the Temple and he had never noticed this hallway. He pulled open the heavy metal door and entered the corridor. The air was stale; it was apparent that this hallway was not a common route for students. Half way to the end, he noticed that there were no doors, that is, only one door at the end. He approached this door and gave it a good push. He did not believe what he saw.

There was simply too much to take in at once. The first thing he noticed was that he knew each and every one of the people standing there. The second thing he saw was Ryan Ridder and Wanda Mardi standing on top of an old, beat up wooden chest. The third thing was the fact that every person in the room was staring at him. Everyone was quiet. Ryan cleared his throat and spoke. "Are you Urumqi?" Without thinking too hard, Oro said "yes." From somewhere in the densely packed room, Oro heard Seth call out. "Would ya quit that Ryan? 'Prolly scared him half to death. He got through the doors, didn't he?" Ryan shot him a disapproving glance. "Viron's spies can get through the doors. They did it once, they can do it again."

At that moment Aan ran up to Oro and grabbed his shoulder. "Scared me to death man, thought you wouldn't make it here," he said kindly. "You didn't miss much, though. I'll give ya a recap. All of us are from Urumqi families. The Empire does not know about us and it needs to stay that way. Ryan and Wanda are our directors." Oro had many questions, but he decided to ask the most important ones first. "Why are they the leaders and how did we all know to come here?" Aan answered his second question first. "It is often very easy for people who are Urumqi to find others like themselves...they just are the leaders...I don't know why." Oro did not like following blindly. Everything he did in life involved a purpose or a reason that he could understand. But it did seem like these people had been given the same speech that he had.

Oro's thoughts were cut short as another person came through the door. He was a tall boy with blonde hair that was longer than it ought to be. "What's up, guys?" he called out before Ryan could use his stupidly serious line. This time, Wanda stepped off of the chest to fill in the newcomer. Although he seemed to fit in fine with everyone, Oro thought that something was different about him. He then realized that this boy was the only person whom he did not know. He went over and introduced himself. "Welcome, man; I'm Oro." The other boy glanced at him. "I'm Derek, Derek Drake." Oro was about to ask him if he was an Urumqi, but he suddenly felt stupid doing so.

Shortly after, five more people came through the door. Oro eyed them carefully. He quickly saw that they were not his friends either; complete strangers. He glanced over his shoulder and saw that Wanda and Ryan were holding their hands above their heads. Everyone began to quiet down. Ryan began. "Now that everyone is here, we can begin. All of you are of Urumqi families. The Urumqi were ancient protectors of Uru. Over the years, our faction has grown less prominent; as the newest generation of Urumqi, it is our job to allow our legacy to continue." A few people started clapping. Oro noticed that Aan was one of them. "As for our true purpose, we cannot yet be sure; but for now, our first priority is to find others like us and bring them here. Once our company grows strong, we may then know what to do." Just as everyone thought it was over, Wanda started talking.

"All of you are to come here every day and show your support to this faction. This includes bringing your staffs; they are your one and only weapon." A slow mumbling was generated. A boy that Oro didn't know called out "What? Are you crazy?" Another girl chimed in "Ya can't get those things past the guards!" Although Oro knew that the staffs could easily be smuggled, he understood their concerns. It had not even occurred to him that he would need his staff. He made a mental note to ask Yia about this. Wanda seemed furious that she had encountered resistance. "Those of you who refuse to cooperate with the rules can leave right now and not ever come back." Even more mumbling erupted from the back of the room. "Hey, who says YOU'RE in charge?" shouted a tall thin boy.

Before things became violent, the bell rang, signaling that the twenty minutes were over. Everyone sprinted down the corridor to their last class. Oro somewhat liked technology. This subject was considered off limits by most Temples because of controversial personal beliefs. In Oro's opinion, any advancement in the way people live their lives was worth discovering. Oro was surprised to see that a handful of students knew far more than him! He wondered if they learned from their parents. Maybe they were allies of the Empire. As their first assignment, the tech students were required to work with the person next to them and categorize the basic elements of technology.

His partner was a rather tall boy with curly black hair. "Hi, I'm Oro," he announced. The other boy was silent for a few seconds. "I'm Dan," he said quietly. Although they completed their assignment with minimal conversation, Oro was happy that he had made a "friend" in at least one of his classes.

Chapter Seven-
Five Groups, Five Newcomers

"Sure is different," declared Seth as the four boys walked home. "Nah, really?" replied Oro, heavy with sarcasm. There wasn't much to talk about. Everything had been said during their secret lunchtime meeting. The four of them were Urumqi, as were nearly all of their friends. No one spoke of Nom. Although finding their 'group' had been easy enough, none of them were in high spirits. Even Seth was rather subdued. Maybe it was because they weren't sure what to do. 'What will happen next?' they wondered.

Oro opened the front door and entered his house. No one was home; no notes this time. They just weren't necessary on weekdays. The Empire required that everyone do their part. All adults were required to work for ten hours a day with little money to show for it. Oro's mother was an accountant and his father oversaw a stone quarry. Like most individuals, they worked for the Empire. It was the only way to earn a good enough living in that age. Even Yia had a job. She watched the local children whose parents worked all day. This was not work to her; she loved every one of those children very much.

He trudged upstairs and set up the ten birch figures. There was no homework to be done, so Kaalah seemed to be the appropriate activity. Utilizing his two generals and one of his captains, he discovered a six move right-checkmate. Oro liked to strategize. It wasn't because he wanted to be in an army; it was just a way to show one's worth. 'Everyone can be a Commander,' he thought. 'We all have our strengths and weaknesses; it is but a matter of finding them, then one's opponent can be beaten.'

The second day was much like the first, as was the third day like the second. The Urumqi lunchtime meetings followed a basic pattern. The first ten minutes were given for everyone to arrive. The remaining ten were entirely consumed by Ryan and Wanda's speeches about finding their purpose. Those who had been more skeptical in the beginning were not enjoying this idle talk. They mumbled and groaned whenever things became too fake.

The first major change happened on the fifth day. Ryan chose to talk about something different. "How many of you have noticed the differences in behavior and attire from one student to the next? Have all of you thought of the categories?" Oro raised his hand. He was surprised to see that almost everyone else did too. He also noticed that the six people he didn't know were the only ones with their hands down. Ryan went on to explain his theory. "There are generally five categories that every person fits into: Traditionals, Contemporaries, Agents, Mandos, and of course the Urumqi. The Traditionals are also known as hill people. They come from poor families with little value placed on education." Ryan's listeners began nodding and muttering. "The Contemporaries have always had their money, but they choose to spend their earnings on themselves, with elaborate clothing and jewelry." More nodding and mumbling came from the group. "The Agents and Mandos are hard to tell apart. Both factions carry weapons, for they are hunters…" "Hunters of what?" called out Seth. "People," answered Ryan.

The side conversations were at a maximum now, each person feeling the need to comment. "They hunt down people for a price. Their client is what makes them different. Mandos find and capture people for the Empire; the Agents do just the opposite." Ryan stepped down from the wooden chest, allowing Wanda to continue the speech. "Traditionally, the Urumqi have been able to make peace with all people… however, the state of things has changed since Vora's death.

In our fight to preserve our faction, we must choose carefully who to ally ourselves with."

All this talk about groups and factions caused Oro to dwell on the five people he didn't know. He decided that it was time to talk to them. He remembered how he had tried to talk to Derek; he would try a different approach. One of the boys was standing by himself. Oro walked over slowly. "Guess we never did end up needing our staffs," said Oro matter-of-factly. The other boy gave a small laugh. "I can't believe how angry she got when Stan asked her why SHE was in charge." "Yeah, Wanda is a little crazy sometimes. I've known her for quite awhile," mused Oro. "I'm Vince Carter," said the boy. He was a rather large kid with thick curly hair. "You know you're the only person that comes here who has bothered to talk to me in the last four days…"

Oro seemed surprised. "You know, now that you mention it…it seems like everybody whose here already knows each other except for you five." He gestured to the others that he didn't know. Vince thought for a moment. "You know, you're right. Everyone was callin' each other by their names from the very first day." Oro wondered what to say. "Well, most of us attended the Temple here to learn, before the Empire gave their order. That's why we all know each other. What Temple are you from?" Vince smiled sheepishly. "My mom is a teacher. She's taught me and my four friends since we were of age," he said, gesturing to the four others that Oro didn't know. "C'mon, I'll go introduce you."

"Hey guys, what's up?" said Vince as he walked up to the others. "This is my buddy Oro," he said, as if Oro was an old friend. "Oro, that's Stan, Jordan, Vicky, and Jim," he declared, pointing at each person. Stan was very tall with thick blonde hair that stuck straight up in the air. Aside from this, he looked a lot like Ja. "Hi," he muttered after Vince was done with his pointing. Jordan was a bit shorter than Stan with long blonde hair. She stood with one hand on her waist as she looked at Oro with her bright blue eyes. Jim and Vicky were almost the opposite: short with brown hair. Jim's was curly and thick, while Vicky's appeared to be smooth. She wore all black; her smile was the only color about her. Oro smiled back. "Why are you people all uptight and stuff?" shouted Jim without even saying hi. Oro just laughed. "I know those two are a little goofy," he said, nodding to Wanda and Ryan, "but the rest of us aren't like that."

At that moment, the bell signaling the start of class rang. The Urumqi grabbed their things and ran to their last class. In Technology, Oro was still thinking about people. It seemed that his partner Dan didn't fit into one of Ryan's categories. Oro wondered if he might be an Urumqi. Maybe he knew Derek. Something was unusual about Derek. 'Derek is the only person who doesn't know anyone!' realized Oro suddenly. He just wasn't sure exactly what that meant.

The next day, Ryan continued his speech about the 'groups'. This time, he started off differently. "Wanda and I have been trying to meet with a representative from each of the groups that I explained yesterday. The Traditionals appear to have no organized rankings, but different factions that are feuding. I'm afraid we will be able to find no allies there. With the Contemporaries we have made a breakthrough. Their leader has given us a proposition. They will stand behind us financially as long as we recognize their social control of this school." Some chatter arose in the back. Oro wondered exactly what he meant by 'control'. Wanda stepped onto the chest. "I'm sure many of you know Dave Datsun. He is the head of the Agents, and will gladly help us under one condition: we are to show him that we are willing to help him stop the Mandos who are interfering with his work. I don't believe that this matter requires a second thought; it is clearly the correct decision."

"I thought that the Urumqi involves the people's decision," called out Stan. "Yeah, you aren't making my social decisions for me!" yelled Vicky. Wanda was furious. "If you don't like the way I run this faction, than you can just leave. ALL OF YOU!" Oro noticed that Aan was slowly making his way over to Stan and Vicky. He followed him, curious to see what would happen. Aan walked up to Stan. "We'd all appreciate it if you'd keep your mouth closed and let them say what they have to say." Stan said nothing; he cocked his eyebrow. Jim was quick to stick up for Stan. "You know what? Screw you, man. You aren't the boss!" he spat. Aan's face grew bright red. "Leave now and don't ever come back!" Jim did just that. He walked through the metal doors without saying another word.

Chapter Eight-
A Difference of Opinion

After school, the four boys were quiet once again. It was as if there was an unwritten rule not to talk about the Urumqi meetings. Oro knew that at some point, he needed to talk to Aan. He knew it would be a mistake to simply 'let go' of an Urumqi. 'What if he joins the Mandos?' he thought. They continued to walk up the hill in silence. "Is it okay if I come by your place for a bit?" said Oro to Aan. "Up to you," he answered.

No one else was in the house. Aan's parents were still at work, and his sister was out with her friends. They sat in the main room, gulping their drinks and talking. "So how come you got so mad at that Jim kid?" said Oro, as if he could care less. "He was messing with Ryan and Wanda. I was getting sick of it; he was ruining it for everybody." "Actually, I thought it was good to hear from someone other than those two. After all, Urumqi should be about the people." Oro could tell that he may have said the wrong thing; Aan was getting angry. "Look: we are in an age of deceit and mistrust. A proper hierarchy is the only way that our faction can get things done. Ryan and Wanda are good leaders and I want to make sure it stays that way." "But why them?" asked Oro suddenly. "Because they're smart," said Aan.

The next day, there were no long speeches. Oro noticed that Ryan and Wanda seemed to be spending their time around the new people. Maybe they were trying to weed out more people, like they had already done to Jim. He had not come back. Derek was not standing by himself. He was right in the middle of all of them, and seemed to suddenly be having a good time. Oro remembered how he had been very quiet in the first few days. Across the room, Ava and Mandi were talking to Zach and Slay. He caught a few words. "...she was one of my best friends. I can't believe she didn't tell me...so how come... her parents are rebels..." Ava was on the verge of tears. He watched as Slay put his arms around her and gave her a hug. The knot that Oro carried in his stomach became a bit bigger.

On the way home, Oro did not talk to Aan. Their relationship was somehow different now. They no longer had the same values. Oro's next thought was to try and find out what Ja thought of the whole thing. Normally, Oro would have talked to Nom, but he had lost him too. "Ja, you want to come over for a bit?" asked Oro. "Sure why not? Its not like I have homework or anything," he said sarcastically.

They went up to Oro's room and Ja unfolded the board. With only two players, Oro found that his new six-move strategy worked even better. The Captain moved two squares forward, and once diagonal. "Wow! I actually won," stated Oro. "It's because I didn't see that move," retorted Ja. They were both quiet for a moment. "Don't you think that there's something's wrong with the Urumqi meetings?" asked Oro. "Like..." "Like how Ryan and Wanda are the 'leaders' or how the new kids don't know anyone or how...how Aan threw Jim out." Ja's face went blank. Oro knew that he didn't see this coming. "Look, Oro, I really don't know; nor do I have the power to make Aan do whatever you want. I'm just trying to go with the flow."

Things were beginning to slowly move forward at the Urumqi meetings; or maybe backward, no one really knew. Oro could tell that everyone was anxious; all wanted to know what would happen next. They soon got their wish. Wanda stepped onto the wooden chest. This time, Ava was by her side. "I have an important announcement," called out Wanda. "One of Ava's friends is in need of our help. I'm sure many of you already know Jade Hira...her family operated a manufacturing company that sold goods to the enemies of the Empire. Both of her parents are dead. The Empire has a reward of 25,000 coins to anyone who captures her. If we do not intervene, every Mando in the school will be after her."

Everyone was quiet. This was rare, considering that Wanda was the one talking. Seth glanced at Ja, who looked over to Oro, who was looking at Vince. Nobody understood what was happening. 'Why are we so worried about the Mandos? It's the Empire that's causing us this trouble,' thought Oro. Ava was crying again. And somehow, Slay was there, telling her that it would all be okay. Aan and Wendy were talking quietly in the corner, as were Vicky and Jordan. They all knew that tomorrow would be quite different. As the bell rang, Ryan reminded everyone to bring their staffs. The first march of the Urumqi was about to begin.

Chapter Nine-
A Different Urumqi;
A Different Oro

When Oro walked through the doors, he saw Ryan and Wanda standing on the wooden chest with their staffs beside them. He was surprised to find that most everyone had brought their staffs as well. In fact the only people who didn't were Vince's group and Derek. "Quiet everyone. Our task will soon be at hand…" Wanda stopped as she heard a knocking on the outer door that connected the hallway to the Great Circle. Aan rushed to answer it. Oro looked down the hallway and saw a smallish boy urgently relaying a message to Aan. "They're planning their attack in five minutes. We need to hurry if we aim to stop them," said Aan importantly. As the Urumqi marched through the doors and down the hallway, Ryan stopped and told Vince that he and the others ought to wait here because they had no weapon to fight with.

Jade sat alone in the hallway reading. Ryan and Wanda were each standing at opposite doors. The others, including Oro, were spaced throughout the hallway. Dave Datsun, now leader of the Agents, stood ready a few feet away from Jade. A few other Agents roamed the hallway, pretending to be looking for their friends. The Mandos attack came quickly and was clearly well planned. Six armored spearmen sprinted down the hallway from each end. Dave looped a cable across one end of the corridor, tripping up three of them. Ja leaped out of nowhere and tripped another with his staff. Seth then stole his spear and charged the other two. He knocked one of them completely out of the hallway, and a blow to the head from Ryan finished the other one.

Six more men entered the hallway. They carried long curved swords, and they were obviously more skilled than their predecessors. Dave held one of them back with his own sword. The thin messenger boy was armed with a bow and targeted a swordsman in the head. Ava's staff tore off a piece of the wall, taking her attacker by surprise. Oro remained with Jade, and it was a good thing he did. Out of nowhere, the ceiling crumpled down on them and the Mando captain jumped down and grabbed Jade. Oro chased after him. Oro leapt at him, his staff striking the captain's heel. All three fell to the ground. The captain pulled out a scimitar and slashed wildly at Oro. Just in time, Oro grabbed his staff and blocked a direct hit from the sharp edged weapon. Ordinary wood would have splintered into a thousand pieces, but Oro's staff stood strong. Jade had just enough time to scramble out of the way. Oro leapt up and struck the captain back. Ryan delivered another blow just in time, for the Mandos and their captain fled in defeat.

"Are you okay?" asked Oro, feeling bad that he didn't completely protect her. "I'm fine," she said. She suddenly threw her arms around him and started crying. "You saved me Oro. If only you could have been there when they came for my parents…" Thinking about her family made her cry even more. The bell rang and the hallway quickly became more crowded. She let go of him slowly. "Could you take me home today, Oro? I don't want them to come after me again." "They won't come back. Not after what I did to their captain!" She smiled a bit. "I'll meet you in the Circle after class, Jade," he agreed.

"I think it's so great how all of you have agreed to work together to stop the Empire," said Jade as the two of them walked home. Oro was glad that someone understood the importance of what he did. "To tell you the truth, we don't exactly work well together. It seems like all we do in our meetings is argue." "That can't be true; you all worked together to help me." "Well you can thank Ava for that. She really cares about you." It seemed that Jade didn't know what to say. "So I guess you like Ryan then, because he makes all of us 'fit together'," said Oro jokingly. "Actually I think he's rather judgmental of everyone. If it wasn't for Ava, I doubt he would have helped me at all...Ava told me about those new kids...and how that Jim kid was kicked out...it's so wrong to just exclude him after one disagreement" Oro was surprised that she knew this much. "You know, you couldn't be more right. I'm just afraid he's gonna join up with those Mandos. I would never want to fight one of my own kind." *'My own kind',* thought Oro.

When they reached Jade's house, everything looked dark. He couldn't imagine coming home to his house knowing that he was the only one left. She opened the door, and then looked back at Oro. "Thanks for everything." He wanted to ask her if she'd like some company, but he decided not to. "Bye, Oro." "Bye."

As he walked home, Oro thought about his own father. He was right to fear the Empire. Viron had the power to simply tear apart families just because they resorted to helping the rebels. He thought some more about Jim. Oro knew that Jim saw the same faults in the Urumqi that he did. He wondered how long it would take for Vince and the others to see it too.

The day after the battle, Ryan was quick to congratulate everyone on their cooperation and performance. He also apologized for not allowing Vince's group to come along. "All you have to do is bring your staffs; no hard feelings. You do have staffs, don't you?" Oro had never thought about this before. Just because they were Urumqi didn't mean that they had all been given their own staffs. Although Vince and his buddies nodded their heads, Derek stood silent. Something was different about Derek, but no one knew what.

Oro walked home with Jade after school. He found out that she knew as much about their happenings as he did. "I don't think that a staff should make that big a difference," she said. "It's just another thing that causes people to get left out." "Yeah," said Oro. "Some families might not let their kids have their own staff. After all, even the Urumqi are afraid of the Empire." He could tell he said the wrong thing. Jade wiped a tear from her eye. When they reached her house, she stopped and looked at Oro. "Do you wanna stay for awhile? It's kinda lonely staying in there by myself," she said, with a nice grin playing across her face. "I'd love to," he answered.

The place was pretty big. Whatever trouble Jade's parents had gotten into, it must have paid off pretty well. They walked into the kitchen. "You want something to eat?" she asked. "No thanks," said Oro politely. In reality he was very hungry, because no one ate during Urumqi meetings. There wasn't a rule against it, but no one had the guts to try it. As for why he said no, he didn't think it would be proper for him to eat her food when he didn't even know if she'd have enough for herself.

They made their way upstairs, only to find more unique things that Oro had never seen before. The first thing that caught his eye was a large table with smooth stone dominos spread out on top. She showed him how the game was played. A player could move a number of his colored stones to certain places on the board. Then a domino is hit which sets up a chain reaction causing some stones to fall off the table. The winner was the player who pushed off the most stones.

Chapter Ten-
Of Origins and Factions

To Oro, things weren't changing much. But in reality, they were. Ryan was becoming more stressed with each passing day. It seemed that he no longer cared about the Urumqi. His main concern was with his newfound allies: the Agents and the Contemporaries.

Dave Datsun had ostensibly come from nowhere. Now, every Agent in the school knew his name. No one knew exactly why he had succeeded. The idea of Agents had been around for as long as there were Mandos to stop; Mandos had been around for as long as there was an Empire to pay them. Agents of the past had been single units, solitary workers on a mission to find clients who needed protection. Dave had successfully changed the rules. His father was an Agent; his father never took him seriously. Dave was just a crazy kid in his father's eyes. Dave had changed much since his father's death. The silly, goofy Dave that everyone liked so much had all but disappeared. Dave Datsun was now the leader of the Agents Clan.

The Clan sought to round up the Agents of the school and unite them so that they could offer more complete protection to those willing to pay. Although his idea was successful, his progress of recruiting was slow. Dave did not have enough people to protect his clients and search for other Agents at the same time. This is where the Urumqi came in. Dave had always been on good terms with Ryan. Now that they were both leaders, they had made an agreement to help each other. Both factions had incompetent numbers to deal with the hand they were dealt. There were currently seventeen Urumqi and even fewer Agents. Dave's plan was working. The Agents and Urumqi were slowly being fused into one.

The Agents were not the primary cause of Ryan's stress. Wanda had made the deal with the Contemporaries. Ryan was the only person who knew. Although both of them agreed that they had made the right decision, the way things would go from now on was not entirely under their control.

The Contemporaries were the largest of the five groups. They were the ones who had the money; it was that simple. None of them were hard workers. Their parents had money; their parents' parents had money. Nothing was there to break the cycle. Contemporaries had money, so they wanted control. To them, Agents and Mandos could be bought and the Traditionals posed no threat, leaving the Urumqi as their only competition. Knowing that the Urumqi were so few, their leader had organized a deal. The Urumqi were to be financially supported by the Contemporaries as long as the Urumqi consulted them before making any major decisions.

Oro no longer paid attention to Wanda or Ryan. He appeared to be listening, but all he thought about was Jade. He had gone to her house after school for about a month now and they had become good friends. Oro wished it could be more, but he wasn't about to push his luck. Jade would never truly understand what it meant to be an Urumqi. And to be quite honest, Oro wouldn't either. Today, things changed a bit. Oro's attention was gained by Wanda when he heard her explain the new 'plan'. "As I have told all of you earlier, the leader of the Contemporaries has offered us a deal. They wish to financially support us as long as we allow them to oversee our budget plans and have a say in most matters of importance."

Almost everyone was listening now. By now, Oro could predict who would go along with this and who would want otherwise. "Why do we need them breathing down our neck?" said Stan as soon as he had the chance. Vicky and Jordan were even more upset. "You knew we didn't want them to be a part of this, but you did it anyway," called out Jordan. "This is absolutely ridiculous. If you've made up your mind not to include us, than we quit!" screamed Vicky. Both of them left. The metal door clanged shut behind them; the Urumqi were now two fewer. Even Stan appeared surprised. Vince just stood there with a look of distress and confusion playing across his face. Seth was the first to break the silence. "She might be right, though. We can't even keep the peace with only seventeen of us! How are we supposed to do it with the Contemporaries watching over our every move?" Almost everyone nodded in agreement "They've already made their decision," said Aan suddenly. "No need to tell me," retorted Seth. "I'm just making a point."

Oro thought about talking to Seth before things got too much worse. But it seemed that he never had the chance. They weren't in any classes together and, since Jade came along, they didn't walk home together either. He knew it was only a matter of time until Ryan would anger Stan to the point of leaving. Then Vince would leave too, and maybe even Derek.

Aan approached the big house. All of the houses in the area were big, but it seemed that only this one was old. Metal decorations lay rusted across the wooden porch. The paint was beginning to peel from the wooden columns lining the walkway. Aside from a few shoes on the porch, the house appeared to be vacant. Aan grabbed the rusty door knocker and tapped it softly. Ryan answered the door. "Come on in; we've been waiting for you." The inside was the complete opposite. Everything was excessively clean and there was absolutely no rust. In the foyer, Wanda sat waiting. After the small talk, Ryan began. "Thank you for coming, Aan; it really does show your loyalty." "No problem," he answered. "I am a bit worried, Aan. Although Wanda and I are glad that you have been enforcing our rules, aren't you worried about what will happen to those Urumqi who have left?" It was Wanda's turn. "Our parents have told us nothing of those who refuse to follow. We thought all the Urumqi would be as cooperative as you."

Aan was happy to receive a compliment, but he didn't let his surprise show. "I wouldn't worry about them, Ryan. They have a much harder time walking through those doors each day than we do. They are weak." "What about their leader, Vince? If Stan walks out on us too, Vince will surely leave with him, and the five of them could cause some serious problems." Aan was ready for this point as well. "Vince is not a strong leader. As long as none of our boys join up with him, they won't ever have the upper hand on us." Wanda and Ryan looked at each other. "That's what I was hoping to talk about, Aan...let's face the facts: all of us Urumqi are either part of your group, or part of mine. I know that my people are loyal. Can you be sure about yours?" Aan was taken aback, but the two others couldn't tell. "That's what I was going to ask you, Ryan. I'm a bit worried about Oro. I know that he sees the problems that are festering within our faction. If he and his boys join up with Vince, they could pose a serious threat to the order." "His boys?" asked Ryan. "I'm talking about Seth and Ja. I don't know if they'll look to me or to Oro if things get bad." Wanda spoke up. "Well, I guess that's the deciding factor. You need to have a serious talk with those two and make sure that they stay with the Urumqi, even if it means that we need to make a few sacrifices." No one talked for a few minutes. "Alright then. Good seein' you Ryan," said Aan as he stood up and walked down the hall.

Aan decided to go to Wendy's. There was really nothing else to do. He wasn't used to doing nothing after school; he would usually leave his house and either wander around, or stop by his friends' houses. She answered the door with a big smile on her face. He was glad that she could still smile;

she had no impending fear, nothing to hide. "Hey sweetie," said Aan. He gave her a quick hug. They talked for awhile. "So what do you think of Ava and Slay?" asked Wendy once the conversation had turned to relationships. "I really don't know. All I know is that it's killing Oro!" he answered. "Oh, I thought he was into Jade now," said Wendy. "Oh, right," said Aan quietly.

They talked for awhile longer, but as the darkness fell, Aan showed himself to the door. As he was walking home, he heard a familiar voice. 'What do you know? Just the person I wanted to see.' He walked up to Stan, who had been talking to another guy, clearly a Traditional. "Hey Stan, you must know who I am," said Aan nicely. "Yeah..." responded Stan slowly. "I must be getting tired, because it sure seems like you're telling something confidential to this rabble." Although the other boy had just been insulted, he kept quiet. "You're out of your mind," said Stan, now obviously annoyed. Aan's expression did not change. "Look, here's the bottom line. Every one of us wants you gone. You can either leave on your own, or I'll tell the Big Man that you've been giving the rabbles inside information." Stan's face was bright red now. "I ain't afraid of Ryan. Tell that fat kid to give me the message directly next time." "Oh no, I'm afraid that you misunderstood. The Big Man that I'm talking about can do much more to you than Ryan can. The Contemporaries don't like tattletales." Aan walked away slowly. 'Killed two birds with one stone,' he thought.

Chapter Eleven-
The Conspiracy

The next meeting began with complete mayhem. Apparently, the rumor had gotten out that Aan had threatened Stan to leave or else he would tell the Contemporaries that Stan was dealing inside information to the Traditionals. Seth was rushing around asking everyone what they knew. Derek just stood and watched everyone scramble around, relating what they did and didn't know. Vince seemed to believe the entire story, backing everything that Stan said. After several minutes more of gossiping, Ryan finally was able to keep everyone quiet. Everyone wanted to know if Aan had really said the things that Stan had claimed. Aan climbed on top of the chest and addressed everyone as a whole. "I personally will deny everything that Stan has accused me of saying. I think that it is obvious to most of you that Stan is trying to retaliate against me because I was the one who had to enforce the rules and get rid of his friends. By no means am I trying to undermine you, Ryan. I was only trying to enforce your rules." Aan quickly looked over at Ryan who was whispering to Wanda. "I think they'll buy it, don't you?" Ryan then stopped short when he noticed that Oro was watching him.

Aan continued his speech about how he would never openly tell a lie, especially to the Urumqi. When Aan was finished, it was Ryan's turn. "To further address your concerns, I must say that I was indeed fully behind Aan's decision to banish Jim Lars for his insolence. I must also remind everyone that accusations of any kind, especially within the Urumqi, will be taken seriously; consequently false accusations will not be tolerated from anyone." By now Stan was fuming. 'How could they just let Aan get away with threatening and conspiracy?' Ryan was far too busy to notice Stan. He was worried about Oro. 'What if he had heard the whisper to Wanda? What if he leaves too?' He remembered what Aan had told him. *Oro isn't a threat as long as his boys stay loyal to me.* 'I guess it doesn't matter. I just hope that Aan is right.'

"So do you think Aan really said those things?" asked Jade as she and Oro walked home. Oro didn't know what to tell her. "Well...I'm not really sure. Aan's been my friend for a real long time...but it does seem like something he would do." "That's not exactly being a good friend," teased Jade. "I guess you had to be there when I saw the hate in his eyes...when he threw out Jim." Jade was taken aback by his comment. When they reached her house, she stopped, looked at him, and smiled. "I think it'd be best if you forgot all about them." Silence. Oro had no idea what to say. It seemed to be a sensitive subject at the moment. "Oh, let's just play some dominos or something." The tension was broken.

Meanwhile, Aan, Seth, and Ja walked home along the West Road. "Can you believe the nerve of that Stan! He tried to accuse me of lying even after I told everyone the truth." "Well, I'm sure everyone believes you," answered Ja. Seth asked, "Are you sure that his accusation was just random? Have you ever even talked to Stan before today?" Aan laughed. "What? Have you been listening to Oro?" Aan intentionally paused. "I think that he doesn't believe me..." The other two boys didn't know what to say. Aan continued, "I think he might choose to leave because of this." "Wow...I never would have expected you and Oro to disagree," said Seth. "Yeah, I know what you mean," said Aan. "I just hope the two of you don't go crazy WITH him," joked Aan. In reality it was no joke at all. Aan needed to hear their answers. "Don't worry about me," said Ja. "I don't exactly fit in anywhere else."

Aan approached an even bigger house. The guard who opened the door was dressed in uniform. He carried a sword at his side, and probably even more weapons that remained unseen. He led Aan to a huge room where the Master of the house sat waiting. The guard left. Aan noticed two more guards on either side of the Master. Their swords were similar to the first guard's, except the edges were jagged and stained with blood. Aan wasn't surprised. The Big Man had many enemies. "Hello. I am Aan Huila of the Urumqi. We are friends of the Contemporaries." "Go on," answered the Master. "I have come to inform you that I believe there is a spy within our ranks. I must ask you what I should do." "I don't know why Wanda doesn't tell me in person, but I believe she has mentioned you, Huila. I believe that you should let me take care of the problem. I will hire a band of Agents to get rid of your spy." "His name is Stan Mitchel. Your Agents can find him in the Great Circle just after the school lunchtime begins." The Master waited. "Very well, Huila. I shall inform your leaders once Mitchel is…gone. Banda!" The guard led Aan to the door.

Oro decided to walk to Yia's. He hadn't seen her in awhile and he decided that it was time for a chat. As he walked up to the door, he saw the last of the summer's flowers. Somehow she was able to keep them blooming longer than anyone else. When he knocked, she opened the large oak door of her cozy home. For the first few minutes, they talked of other matters, inevitably leaving the subject of Urumqi for last. "Yia, there's something I have to ask you. Is there something more to being an Urumqi than just believing in the legend of Ben?" "Oh, of course there is. I thought you already knew this, but the Urumqi of a given generation know each other. They also know some other things too, like where to meet and what the customs are."

Oro thought about that. "That's what I was going to ask you about…there were six people in the beginning who didn't know anyone. Five of them knew each other. The last one knew no one." Yia's expression changed. "That's not good. Only the Guranqi know where you meet." Her expression relaxed a bit. "Oh, I shouldn't say that. I'm sure all of your friends are okay people. Only Urumqi would come to your meetings." "Well it seems that almost everyone agrees with you." "What do you mean?" "Our leader has already thrown out three of them." "Well that's no good either, now is it?" She smiled. "I can't give you all of the answers, Oro. My generation doesn't exactly have much experience. You just need to do what you think is right." "Okay." He gave her a hug and set out for home.

Stan was running late. He had just shoved everything into his book bag and was the last one to leave the classroom. He practically ran to the end of the Great Circle where the metal doors stood. Something was different today. He decided that it would be best to approach the doors slowly. He was wise in doing so. As his hand reached out to push the door aside, an arrow whirred past his head. He quickly looked around and saw a formidable group of Agents, all of them with drawn swords. "That shot was but a warning. The next one will not miss." Stan recognized the thin boy who had fired the arrow. He was Dave's messenger and personal assistant. "I'm not sure how much you claim to know, but by now it should be obvious that things are changing. The Contemporaries, Agents, and Urumqi are slowly becoming one. All three factions want you gone. You will not pass through those doors without a fight." Stan did not flinch at all. In fact, he took two small steps closer to the thin boy. "You know what? I could take each and every one of you apart. But I'm not that much of an idiot. I know how the Big Man runs his show. If I kill you, he will destroy my family and everything else that I love. Tell them good riddance!"

Chapter Twelve- Walked Away

Neither Stan nor the thin boy knew that someone was listening. In fact, the thin boy would never know. Oro retreated behind a stone column just as Stan turned his back and left. Oro knew he had to do something. Now he knew for sure that Aan was lying. His best friend had lied to him. Aan was no longer his best friend; not until a few things were discussed...

In the little room at the end of the hallway, Ryan addressed the group. "It seems that our number is less today. Not one, but two! Not a coincidence if you ask me. It would seem that Stan Mitchel no longer wishes to be known as a liar. As for Oro, I have no idea where he might be," mocked Ryan. This was the first time that anyone had been absent from a meeting. In general, everyone was tense; Vince especially. He sat by himself in the corner, wondering what had happened to his best friend. 'Will they try to threaten me next? Where is Oro? Has Aan gone after him too?' As Vince thought things through, he realized that he no longer had a reason to stay. Every Urumqi who had ever been nice to him was gone. Just as he was about to stand up and announce his departure, Oro burst through the doors. He walked straight to Aan. "You lied to me, Aan. You lied to all of us. You threatened Stan Mitchel into leaving. Your decisions have caused the Urumqi to crumble apart!" Everyone's attention was directed at Oro. "What do you have to say to me, Aan? What are you going to tell us?" Aan's expression did not falter in the slightest. He just stared back at Oro with a false look of sadness on his face.

"I cannot believe that you're serious, Oro. It is sad to think that my best friend has chosen to believe their lies. Don't you get it, Oro? They aren't Urumqi..." "I'M SORRY IF I MISUNDERSTOOD," boomed Vince from the corner. "Are you saying that my friends and I are not worthy of being here? Is that why you kicked us out?" Everyone grew silent. Oro was next to speak. "Tell me, FRIEND, are you judging me as 'not Urumqi' too, because I would hate to think so. You can't win, Aan. It's just like the ancient rule of all government. 'The more you tighten your grip, more people will slip through your fingers'." Aan was clearly beyond words. Slay moved to confront Oro. "Look, we're tired of hearing it. Just get out..." Oro's blow to Slay's jaw was more than enough to stop him in mid sentence. As Slay fell, jolts of blue electric crackled about his body. Oro and Vince retreated to the door.

"Well, I finally did it. I left," said Oro seriously. "Huh?" "I left the Urumqi." Jade's playful expression vanished. "But...why?" Oro really didn't know what to tell her. He was afraid she'd be upset, but he knew it would be wrong not to tell her. "A lot of reasons...But I really don't wanna talk about it, okay?" "No. I deserve an answer." Silence. "Look, there were just too many rude and judgmental people. I just couldn't take it anymore...not to mention my best friend, who lied to my face!" "Are you sure you aren't talking about yourself Oro?" "Aw Jade, why are you doing this? I already feel guilty enough for leaving. I don't need it from you too." "Well what does that mean? Are you just going to leave me too?" Oro stopped and looked her in the eyes. "No, Jade. That's why I wanted to tell you the truth. Every other guy would have hid the truth...but not me" "It's no good talking now. You've already made up your mind. It wasn't *you* who saved me, Oro. It was the Urumqi." A tear rolled down her cheek. "Only bad people leave the Urumqi. I'm sorry Oro." She began to walk away. "Is that what your parents said, Jade? Only bad people leave? Well they're dead now. Shows you how much they knew!" Just after he said it, he knew he had said too much. She would never forgive him for that.

Oro walked home alone, and in silence. He had tons to think about. It was unbelievable that his best friend had lied to his face. Aan Huila would pay for that before things were through. He thought of Ja and Seth. 'They will never know the truth.'

Walked away; heard them say:
Poisoned hearts will never change
Walked away again.
Turned away in disgrace,
Felt that chill upon my face
Cooling from within.

Chapter Thirteen-
The Imperial Scheme

That night, Emperor Viron paced his father's halls. He stopped at the headstone that read "Keep your friends close; keep your enemies closer ~ Vora". 'Poor old man', he thought. 'If only you had listened to your own words, you might have ended your life in glory.' He continued down the hall until he reached the rough metal door. With a wave of his hand, the door shot upward. "Rise, my son." A cloaked figure slowly stood. "What news have you for me?" The hooded one lowered his cowl. "Your plans have been set in motion, father, with very little help from me." They now walked together back down the hall. "It is what I have foreseen." "The Urumqi will fight and quarrel until only Kanoka is left. This fight is as good as won," said the son. Replacing his coarse hood, he proceeded back towards the throne room door.

Part Two- The Storm

Chapter One- The Stories

Few folk of Uru knew what would come of today. Oro Kanoka was no longer a part of the Urumqi. Ja Kahn and Seth Andora were living a lie. Wanda Mardi and Ryan Ridder stood on their chest of gold, waiting for the next opportunity to raise their personal status. Dave Datsun paced his room, telling himself not to fail his father. Slay Ander acted similarly, thinking about Ava Bera, who was walking the West Road with Mandi Shale to school. Vince Carter was shutting his eyes, hoping to wake up in a different world. Stan Mitchel and Jim Lars were play fighting in the road in front of their houses. Jordan Lia and Vicky Marah were fast asleep. Dan Carver was eating breakfast; his thoughts dwelled on the small gizmo that he was fiddling with. Jade Hira was sulking around her room, not quite sure of how she was feeling. And worst of all, Aan Huila was preaching to Wendy about how every aspect of life would be better without Oro. She wasn't really listening.

As Oro walked to school, he thought about where to go. Ever since he had arrived at his old Temple, he had been drawn to that hallway. 'What now?" Lunchtime soon came, and Oro set out on an aimless walk, hoping to find a familiar face. His path soon took him to the center of the Great Circle, where he found Vince, Stan, Jim, Jordan, and Vicky all looking at him. "What do you want?" said Jim, with his overly aggressive voice. Oro quickly thought of what to say. "I just wanted to say that you were smart to leave..." This answer seemed to satisfy everyone. "...and that I guess I'm one of you now." "You bet, man," said Vince, quickly coming to his rescue. No one talked for a bit.

"So what are we going to do now?" inquired Oro. Everyone laughed. "Well, we now know what the QUESTION is, but how about that answer," said Vince sarcastically. Stan replied, "Well, usually we tell the new guy our story, I guess. You are only the second one, so it's not exactly a tradition." Oro could tell that Stan was trying to be funny, but in an underlying way. "Alright," said Oro. He looked around; he noticed that everyone was walking around the six of them, as if they weren't even there. "Hey...can everyone else hear what we're saying? We aren't in a secretive room like before." "Urumqi don't need walls to keep others from listening," said Jim with conviction. "No one could find us right now even if they tried." "Impressive," nodded Oro.

As Stan began his story, the six of them knew that it was time to listen. "The first thing that you should know is that my family is big. No, more like huge; I am the youngest of nine. My parents are really into their jobs, so it was up to the other eight Mitchels to raise me. My dad is a cartographer; mom is a sculptor." His smile widened as he reached the interesting part of his story. "I was always told that I was different. I was told never to fear anyone; I was the one that others would fear. Thinking that way worked for me I guess; I've never had any doubt in my mind that I was doing the right thing. Whenever I was sad, I'd tell myself I was different, and that everything would be okay." Oro asked, "Are all of your brothers and sisters Urumqi too?" Everyone looked at him. "HA!" exclaimed Jim. "Only the youngest in a family becomes an Urumqi," offered Vince. Oro wasn't yet sure what that would mean. The bell rang. Oro felt like he had just got there! During technology, he thought about his new friends. 'Everything *will* be okay,' he thought.

The next day, it was Jim's turn. "When I was born, my mother and father weren't together." He seemed relieved to have finished the sentence. "Just after, my mother died. I've been with my step-dad ever since. I don't think he really cares about me... I was just a regular kid until I met Stan. He offered to take me to the Carter school, so I went. Just after he had been trained as an Urumqi, we got in a fight about something. He jumped at me with his staff and I blocked him. Since then, everyone's known I was an Urumqi." At this point, Jim was really enjoying his story. Oro spoke up. "So all of you really do have staffs? How come you were so reluctant to bring them?" Vicky answered, "Traditionally, we only fight when we have no other choice." "Ryan tried to use us as soldiers. We knew well enough to refuse," added Jordan. "Well you were smarter than I was," joked Oro. The bell sounded from atop the wall. "Hey, where you goin Oro?" asked Jim. "Technology." "Me too, I'll go with ya."

"You didn't say what you're dad does," pointed out Oro as they walked to class. "Well...he's an overseer for the Empire," answered Jim awkwardly. "I don't exactly enjoy bringing that up..." As they walked down the Technology hall, Oro saw Dan. Jim called out, "Danny, what's up man?" "Hi," said Dan quietly. "I guess you two know each other," confirmed Oro. Jim explained, "Yeah, Dan's been my buddy for awhile now. Actually, he's part of our group but he doesn't come all the time. By the way, where were you today?" Dan seemed excited to tell. "I was out back working on a new capsule for that powder I was telling you about." "Nice," said Jim. "Can't wait to hear about it. I gotta get going." He jogged a ways down the hall to his next class.

"So are you an Urumqi?" asked Oro once he was alone with Dan. "No," said Dan. "But I don't really fit in anywhere else." Oro laughed. "I know what you mean. People at this place don't exactly make fitting-in easy." They walked into the classroom. "So you're really into tech stuff?" asked Oro. "Yeah, my dad's one of the best, or so he says; he's been teaching me the basics, that's all." Dan smiled. "Dad actually thinks he's ahead of the Empire in some ways…" Oro was surprised to hear Dan say that after how modest he had been about his own skills. "Really?" "Yeah…That capsule I was telling Jim about…it could bring about a completely new way of fighting by simply using fire." The bell rang, cutting short their conversation.

Tomorrow soon came, for it was Vince's turn to tell his story. "I don't really have much to tell you, Oro," offered Vince. "My mom is the Urumqi of my family and she's overprotective. So much so that she decided to home school me. That was when I met Stan; his family and ours were long time friends. And then of course you already know about Jim… Jordan, go ahead and tell yours." She hesitated. "Okay." She swished her hair back, getting Stan's attention. "My parents aren't together either. When my mom found out that my dad was an Urumqi, she didn't wanna be with him anymore. Since then, it's been all up to dad to raise me and my sisters." There was an awkward silence. "Don't take that lightly; her sisters are mean!" confirmed Vicky. They all had a good laugh.

"I need to talk to Dan," said Jim after the bell rang. They walked down the Tech hall. "We ought to make sure that we buy his new fire thing before anyone else." Oro was confused. "You mean you buy his inventions?" "Not really; all we're buying is the technology. Eventually, new inventions leak out. It's because of the Empire, because of people like my dad." Oro didn't know how to answer. Jim glanced into Oro's classroom. "I don't think he's here today. Probably busy working."

That night, Oro wondered about money. He had never really thought much about it before. All he knew was that most everyone was poor and that his family was lucky to have enough. He wondered where Jim and the others got the money to buy Dan's technology. The small group of outcasts had become like a family, and he was their newest member. The Urumqi should have been Oro's family, but they weren't. All they cared about were their meaningless alliances and treaties with powerful figures like the Big Man. They were not a family; come time, they would lose.

Chapter Two- The Blasters

Once the six of them met in the center of the Great Circle, it was Vicky's turn. Before she could begin, Dan strode over carrying what seemed to be a long tube with a handle. "GO AWAY!" yelled Vicky before Dan could speak. Nobody could tell if she was kidding or not. "Calm down, Vicky," said Stan smiling. "So...let's see it, Dan," said Jim. Dan pulled out a small oblong capsule from the tube. "The stuff in here is a new kind of chemical that I've created using various woods and metals. The result is a powder that causes air to expand rapidly when heated. This powder has opened up a whole new area of Technological Science. However, the use that I'm sure you will find most interesting lies in this tube. If I put this capsule full of the powder into this tube and light it on fire," he explained, indicating the small fuse attached to the capsule, "the rapid expansion of air inside the tube will force the capsule out the other end. The force is about three times that of an arrow, not to mention the sharpened point of the capsule being much larger than an arrowhead."

They were all impressed with his explanation, but no one save Jim was quite sure that the whole contraption would work. "Want me to try and demonstrate?" asked Dan jokingly. "No, I'd rather you didn't," answered Jordan. "There's a chance that someone might get hurt." Dan laughed. Oro enjoyed the sense of humor that they had all grown used to. In fact, no one ever really told a joke, but the ridiculousness of the matter of fact statements more than did the job. The clanging from atop the wall left Vicky with no time for her story. "So can you make six of these by tomorrow?" asked Jim. "I'll try," was Dan's skeptical response.

For some reason, Oro didn't feel like going home. It used to be that he could just stay at Aan's or Seth's place for awhile; now things were different. He thought about Nom. Perhaps it was time to go see him. He turned off after passing through the gate and found the East Road. Nom's house was old and rustic, but still had within it a glowing light of warmth. He knocked on the door. "Hi, is Nom there?" "One minute…" "Oro!" shouted Nom as soon as he saw his friend. "How's it goin', man?" returned Oro. They walked out to a trail behind the house. "So, do I dare ask if you're an Urumqi?" said Oro with a grin. "You bet." "I suppose you're the leader at your school?" "Huh?" "Aren't you the leader of all the Urumqi?" asked Oro.

Nom looked confused. "There are only two of us: it's just me and Mac Kalomo." Oro's expression faltered slightly. "Why, is that a bad thing?" asked Nom when he noticed. "At this point, I don't know, buddy…There's a lot that's been goin' on. Aan has tried to undermine the Urumqi leaders." As Oro continued, Nom's eyes grew wide. "Six of us have left the main order and started somewhat of a resistance. We may need your help." "Well, it seems like you've got your hands full." Nom's serious expression split into a smile. They had a good laugh. "I'll see you around buddy… maybe a bit sooner than you think."

Finally, Vicky's turn came. "Dad is one of his generation's leaders, or so he says. He's told me that everyone can be a leader if they set their mind to it. That advice hasn't really worked though…" "I know what you mean," interjected Oro. "Dads are all talk." Vicky smiled. He had never seen her truly smile before. Or if he had, he didn't remember. She was beautiful. Not in the same way as Jordan, but in a more unique way. She continued her story. "I have an older brother; I think he's dad's favorite, but I'm not really sure…dad probably wishes I was a boy too. Anyway, he used to be involved with the Empire. When they found out that he had special powers, they forced him to work for them full time. He refused, and then escaped from their grasp. Ever since, they've tried to come after him. They never succeed, of course, but sometimes I can't help but wonder…What if they get fed up? What if they try to kill him?"

Her dramatic ending was interrupted by Dan. "GO AWAY," she shouted as usual. Oro noticed that Dan was wearing an unusually big trench coat. The Urumqi typically wore shorter brown jackets with plain shirts and baggy pants. Jim was quick to ask, "What's up with the jacket?" "I used it to get your blasters through security," said Dan excitedly. "Blasters?" asked Jim. "Yeah, the fire-arrows. That's my new name for them. Anyway, I got six of them all ready. Do you have the cash?" He looked over at Stan. "Depends," he replied. "How much you want for each one?" "How 'bout 100." Stan reached into his own coat pocket and pulled out six roles of 100 coins each. "There you go, man. Hand over the blasters." Dan pulled them out of his trench coat one by one and handed one to each of the five. The ringing of the bell mollified their excitement. As Dan walked away with his cash, Oro asked Stan, "How are we going to get these things OUT of security?" Stan smiled. "Smuggling is my specialty. Just wait and see." "So are we all going to meet at the gate after last class?" asked Oro. "Sounds like a plan," said Vince. He turned to Oro. "Remind me to tell you about the cash…"

During technology, Oro thought about Nom and Mac. He knew that Jim and the others wouldn't exactly get along with them. His new friends were so dark and indifferent toward outsiders. He remembered Mac's lively greeting at the party when they first met. Jim would have definitely criticized him. Oro's thoughts drifted to the Empire. It was surprising to him that the Empire did not know that the Urumqi were primarily at West side school[1]. Or maybe they did. Maybe the Empire was plotting against him at this very moment…

Chapter Three- The Power of Urumqi

After technology, Oro met up with Vince and the others at the wall. "Watch me," said Stan as he approached the guard. "What's that?" asked the guard boisterously. "Huh?" answered Stan. Oro couldn't believe it. Stan's blaster had just vanished before the guard's eyes! The guard was so befuddled that he allowed Stan to pass without any further questions. The others did the same, each at a different gate as not to draw attention. When it was Oro's turn, the guard tried to grab his blaster. It vanished. "Watch your hands!" said Oro to the guard. A confused look was all he received in return.

"Pretty good for your first time," said Vince, as he pulled his blaster out from under his shirt. Stan's simply floated in mid-air behind his back. Jim's was behind his coat. "So how were we able to do that?" asked Oro. "Your *will* for the blaster to be hidden from the guard was great enough that your mind was able to hide it for you," explained Stan. They walked together along the West Road. "How 'bout we all come by my place," suggested Jordan. "I have the place to myself." She smiled and looked at Stan.

The six of them slouched into the chairs that took up much of Jordan's family room. She grabbed a pack of drinks and some junk to snack on. The 'first course' was gone almost instantly. As Jordan went to grab more, Stan jokingly called out, "I think I spilled!" "You better not have," yelled Jordan from the kitchen. "Here, you better take this, just in case I spill again," said Stan, throwing her his open drink. She caught it, and threw it back playfully without spilling any. "Alright now, let's not have a food fight…" "But that would be so much fun," interjected Jim. "Hey, I just got a Kaalah board if you're interested," announced Jordan. "Maybe that'll calm everyone down," added Vicky. As the least experienced of the group, Jordan and Vince decided to let the other four play. Oro took a seat next to the birch figures. Across from him was Vicky, toying with the mahogany pieces. Jim's pine Commander suffered an early defeat. Oro played defensively, waiting for Stan's ash pieces to weaken Vicky's force.

As an experienced player, it was obvious to Oro that the only way he would lose was if Vicky and Stan chose to work together. It seemed to Oro that Stan was thinking the same thing. Vicky moved her mahogany Captain. "That's mate, Stan," she said in an evil voice. What'd you do that for?" exclaimed Jim. "Without your ally you'll lose!" Oro moved his center soldier forward. "Game," he said quietly.

Jordan broke the silence. "We still don't know our purpose, do we? Why are we all together? What are we supposed to do?" No one spoke. "You know…I've wondered the same thing myself," said Vince slowly. "But I think I do know why we are together." Everyone was listening. "We all have something that we fear. I fear that because my parents are overprotective, they won't let me do what is necessary to become an Urumqi. I fear that I might have failed as a leader." "I know what you mean," said Stan, "and you haven't failed us; at least not yet anyway. But you're right. I'm afraid that the things my family told me were wrong. Jim's afraid of the Empire, afraid of people like his father." Jordan took over. "I worry about my family, my future. What if people abandon me because of what I believe?" She paused. "I know Vicky's afraid that her dad's past will catch up with him…What about you Oro? What are you afraid of?" All eyes were on him. "I'm afraid that people like Aan Huila are gonna corrupt all the good people in this world and then I'll have nobody!" He didn't plan to come on so strong; it just happened.

Yia had just finished sweeping her front porch. The last of the summer's flowers had died. She hated cleaning up the dead petals; it reminded her that she would have to wait until spring when the new ones would sprout. She decided to take a walk; she needed to go visit an old friend. She approached the Patal house and knocked on the door. She hugged the old lady who answered the door. The old lady was Nom's grandmother. The two of them walked out to the trail. "It's been so long; I'm sure there are a million things to discuss," beamed Yia. "Ha, yeah. What with all the new Emperor and such. 'Wish our generation could have overthrown them when we had the chance." They chatted for awhile, but ultimately, the subject was somehow changed back to the Urumqi. "I don't think our children turned out as good as we would have liked," mused Nom's grandma. "I know what you mean," agreed Yia. "It's not right that Oro has to grow up without an Urumqi parent...." "So Oro is an Urumqi?" asked Mrs. Patal. "Yes." Silence. They headed back toward the house. "I just have to say that I am so sorry to hear about your son," said Mrs. Patal. "I wish I would have been there...you must have been devastated." Yia looked at her old friend. "Let's not talk about him."

The Big Man sat on his throne, watching the five people below him. He loved strategy. The idea of moving pieces slowly, one at a time, to ultimately create the desired effect, was a skill that, in his mind, was beyond compare. The others that were before him were, in a way, all under his control. Aan Huila, Ryan Ridder, Wanda Mardi, Dave Datsun, and the thin boy all waited anxiously to see what the Master would say. "Well, Wanda, is everything going as planned?" "Yes, sir. The money you have provided us with has allowed Dave to recruit enough Agents to create more effective protection for those willing to pay." She acknowledged Dave, who nodded slowly. Ryan spoke. "I assume you have encountered little opposition to your social control of things?" The Master smiled. "Yes, that's what we must talk about. It seems that the Traditionals have found a way to intercept a great deal of my goods before they reach the various businesses that I cater to. You must find a way to stop them or else I will be unable to continue the financial support of your faction."

Aan did not like what he heard. He stepped much closer to the Master's chair. "We do not have sufficient numbers to take on the Traditionals. We will need your coins if we are to carry out your request." "GET HIM BACK!" commanded the Master. A guard stepped forward and raised his ridged sword. Aan did not move. As the guard struck, Aan pulled out his staff to block the blow. Just as quickly, he impaled the guard with no apparent effort. "I think we understand each other," said Aan. "I am the Master now."

Oro finally understood his purpose. No one else was going to go up against Aan. He had to be the one. He also understood something else. He understood fear. Fear can be used to create anger; within anger lies great power. He walked alone through the rusty rotten dust that was known as the West Road. Summer was almost over, and the first rains of autumn were yet to begin. As he entered the Great Circle, he noticed a change. The lazy nature of the people had become tenser. He couldn't tell what the difference was until Vince pointed it out that day at lunch. "The Mandos are restless today," observed Vince. "I bet they're planning something really big." Silence. "I know what they're planning," said Vicky with a peculiarly quiet voice. "They're coming after my dad." None of them, not even Vince, knew what to say. Tears began to form in her eyes. Oro put his arm around her; he held her close until she was feeling better. "You have nothing to worry about," he whispered to her. "We're all gonna come by you're place after class and show those Mandos not to mess with the Urumqi! Am I right?" The others nodded in agreement.

Across miles of dusty road, Nom sat talking with Mac as the bell rang. Nom grabbed his things and set off to class. On the way, he bumped into Max Toko, and had an idea. "Hey Max, how have you been?" beamed Nom. "Alright, I guess," answered Max. Max Toko was the leader of a formidable group of Agents at the East side school[2]. "Hey, did you hear that the Mandos of West side are getting ready for something?" asked Nom. "Actually, I've got a few contacts down there. I did hear." "You know I'm planning on heading down there myself this afternoon," said Nom matter-of-factly. "Why don't you and some of your buddies tag along?" "Alright, why not," replied Max as he walked away.

Nom knew that he had potential as an Urumqi. Not necessarily as a warrior, but as a thinker. After all, the Urumqi powers begin with the mind. No one told Nom about the Mandos at the West side school; He just knew. It was like his grandmother had taught him: 'The Urumqi can accomplish things using their mind that would take normal men years to achieve…'

Chapter Four-
The Battle in the Canyon

The six of them walked along the road together. No one talked. Oro noticed the familiar look on Vince's face. He remembered it from the time when Vince had spoken out against the Urumqi; he remembered it from the confrontation with Aan. The others were just as somber as their leader. Vicky led the group up a steep hill, and then into a small valley just off the side of the West Road. The house was small and dreary with an old wooden porch rotting away just under the front door. Two men stood there. The older of the two was James Marah, Vicky's father; the younger man was her brother, also called James. The latter was holding a sledge hammer tightly in his fist. Oro and the others approached the old porch. "You'd think after all this time they'd just forget about me," mumbled Mr. Marah. Vicky gave him a quick hug. "So did I bring enough bodies?" she asked. Her dad laughed. "All of them are Urumqi?" "Yeah." For awhile, they all just stood there looking at each other. Each knew that it would be the Mandos who would make the first move.

The first one came alone; he made his way up the hill and into the Valley. There were others with him, of course, but they kept their distance, mostly keeping to the cliffs on the outskirts of the Valley. Oro recognized the first one as the Mando captain who had led the attack on Jade. The captain walked slowly but steadily toward the porch. Without saying a word, Vicky's brother jumped from the porch and stepped up to meet him. "I think you might be a bit lost, stranger. This here is private property." He held up the hammer to show that he meant business. "I'm looking for James Marah," said the Captain flatly. "You're lookin' at him," spat James. "Your father," said the Captain, pointing, "I must speak with him. Step aside." James did not falter. "You got something for him, you tell me." Silence. "I said tell me, punk!" James struck the captain with the end of the hammer squarely in the chest. Arrows flew down from the cliffs as the other Mandos witnessed the assault on their captain; the battle had begun.

"Stan! Jordan! Jim! Get to the cliffs and take out those archers! The rest of us can handle the swordsmen," shouted Vince as he sidestepped a few arrows. The Captain had since recovered from the blow, and was now joined by close to forty Mandos carrying various swords and spears. Mr. Marah stepped down from the porch to face his enemies. Without speaking, he whipped out his staff with one hand and shot his other hand quickly forward. A spear flew from the hand of the nearest Mando and landed comfortably into his hand. Without warning, he lunged at the closest group of attackers and began hacking away. Young James and the three remaining Urumqi did the same. This was the first time that Oro had seen his new group's staffs. Vicky's was longer than his and made of a darker wood, with intricate carvings at both the top and the bottom. Vince's was very thick, and had little carving, if any. Together with the Marahs, they began to cut a gap in the line of attackers.

Oro wasn't quite in the fray; he knew that a true Urumqi must look around the battle field to determine the most effective person or place to fight. Out of the corner of his eye, he saw the Captain making his way up the sheer face of the cliff where Stan and Jordan were attacking the archers. He sprinted to the base of the cliff and tried to climb. The Captain was using the metal hooks on his arm guards to pull his way up. There was no way that Oro could follow. But then he remembered Stan's words. 'If your *will* to do something is great enough, it will happen; that is what makes you an Urumqi.' Oro jumped for the nearest precipice. A normal man could have never made the jump, but Oro

Kanoka did. He pulled himself up through the rocks to the ledge where the archers were firing their arrows. He knocked off the nearest one with a kick and proceeded to attack the others with his staff. The Captain was just ahead of him now, making his way toward Jordan. His iron plated glove packed a deadly punch to her back before she heard Oro yell.

Stan saw Jordan's staff slip from her hand as she struggled to grab onto the edge of the cliff. With a speed faster than any creature in Uru, Stan leapt from his ledge and ignited his blaster with a spark from his staff. The shot nearly knocked the captain off of the high cliff. Stan grabbed hold of Jordan's hand and helped her up. Oro had just enough time to pull himself up to the ledge to stop the captain's counter-attack. He rushed at the heavily armored Mando with his staff. The captain parried the first blow with his scimitar, but was not fast enough to block the left-handed punch that Oro delivered to his chest. Blue energy crackled about his body as he fell to the Valley floor.

"Stan, you saved me," sobbed Jordan as she squeezed him tightly. "You didn't think I'd let you fall down there, did you?" joked Stan. Oro was happy for them, but the battle still raged on below. The Mandos had pushed the Marah group away from the house and toward the face of the cliff. Oro knew he didn't have much time. The captain had recovered from his fall and edged toward his enemies. Scimitar in hand, he lunged out at young James. The sharp edge caught him in the shoulder. "No!" screamed Vicky. She arched her staff around behind her, sweeping the captain off his feet. Oro didn't know what to do. If he jumped, he might hurt himself, which could cost them the battle. But if he didn't, his friend might die. Oro took the chance. He leapt from the cliff toward the spot where Vicky was dueling with the captain. He overshot his jump and landed back into the fray of swordsmen.

His knees felt weak. He stumbled to a halt. He could hardly see the gigantic Mando brute that lumbered toward him. "Time to die," said the cold voice. The brute lifted his axe. And then he fell; in his place stood Nom. "Run, Oro!" he yelled. Oro knew where he had to go. He dashed to the dune where Vicky was fighting the captain. It seemed he was too late. His girl stumbled to the ground following a blow to the head. Without time, without contemplation, Oro used his powers to lift up the closest thing to him, a boulder, and hurled it at the captain. The impact cracked the captain's helm and sent him tumbling to the ground.

Chapter Five-
The Compromise

"Fire!" yelled Max. His agents released a flurry of arrows on the attacking Mandos. Many fell back. Mac Kalomo and Nom Patal had joined the brawl, leveling brutes and spearmen with their staffs. Jim's jump from the cliff was a bit more successful than Oro's and he too did his part in defending the Valley. Stan rushed across the ledges and finished off the remaining Mando archers. Below, the Mando attack group was nearly depleted. Mr. Marah rushed over to his son and pulled the broken edge of the scimitar out of his arm. Vince looked around in dismay at the number of Mandos they had destroyed. Oro regained his senses and ran toward Vicky. He knelt down by her side. "Guess you got him, huh?" she said softly. "Nah, I think I just knocked him out." She pulled herself closer to him. "Our group owes you so much, Oro; and I, especially." She gave him that warm smile. Their eyes locked. Their lips touched. "Hey, where is that captain?" boomed Mr. Marah's voice across the canyon. Vicky looked away from Oro. He could tell by the look on her face that she felt uneasy. "We can keep this a secret," whispered Oro. She nodded.

After a few minutes, the rest of the group made their way over to the spot where the captain lay. "Well...what are we gonna do with him?" asked Vince. Everyone looked around. It was obvious that this was the most relevant question, but nobody seemed to have an answer. "Let's just kill him. He doesn't deserve any better," said Jim coldly, as he moved to strike him with the end of his staff. "Wait," shouted Oro, "I have a better idea. This guy is a good fighter. Why don't we hire him to fight for us? He is the link that we need to stop both the Empire and the West side Agents..." "Mandos are dangerous; you can't trust them," spat Jim. "Look, I don't think you understand," persisted Oro. "When we left, the Urumqi had already allied themselves with Dave's Agents. By now, I am sure that Aan Huila has also forced upon them a deal with the Contemporaries. If so, it won't be long before he takes control of all three factions and tries to overthrow us. Without help from these Mandos, we have no allies but the few Agents that have come from the East side."

"I understand what you're saying," said Stan, "but I'm afraid you're forgetting someone." He nodded to Vince, who gave the explanation. "The money that we spent on Dan's weapons was not entirely ours. Stan knows a contact within the Traditionals' ranks. We have been helping the Traditionals to steal cargo from the Big Man's businesses. In turn, we receive a cut of the profits that the Traditionals make when selling these stolen products." "Well that's the answer then," said Oro quickly. "If we use the money to hire this captain's Mandos, we could steal more goods from the Contemporaries and increase our profit." The others gave their general consent. Only the three Marahs stood back. "These people have hunted, harassed, and aggravated our family for my entire life. It is with regret that the Urumqi have split, and with even more regret that we must be the side that relies on the Mandos. So be it," grumbled big James. Oro was surprised that he went along with the plan so well.

"Well, let's try to wake him up." Vince gave the unconscious captain a soft kick. He stirred to life, at first not remembering who or where he was. When it all came back to him, he asked slowly, "Which one of you threw that boulder?" Oro acknowledged himself. "You're a good fighter," he said tersely. The captain examined Oro more closely. "I know who you are; you are the one who faced me when I went after Jade Hira. I suppose only an Urumqi could have caught me off guard like that." The others looked at him skeptically. Oro was surprised at the captain's cocky attitude. It was almost as if he thought that his only competition was someone with special abilities.

"So are you all gonna kill me, or do you have it in your hearts to let me go?" Nobody wanted to answer his question directly, so Oro was forced to do so. "Actually, we have a proposition for you." The captain looked relieved. "Well, I am a man of business. Aaron Brown." He pointed respectfully at Oro. "Oro Kanoka."

Vince cut the salutation short. "With our help, the Traditionals have been able to intercept cargo transports belonging to the Contemporaries. They then sell the stolen goods and we receive a cut of the money. Since the Contemporaries have shown no signs of further security, we would inquire as to whether you and your Mandos could assist us in stealing the products. You would naturally receive a cut of the money after each job is done." He emphasized the word *after*. Mr. Marah broke in, "Should you refuse, you will not live to see another day. Should you agree and not show when the time comes...the hunter will become the hunted." He smiled. Aaron did not appear to be affected by the threat. He stood his ground and stared back at the others. "One more thing," said Jim. "No more jobs for the Empire. You 'work' for us now. I trust that there are enough Mandos to serve you and the Empire without causing an upset?" "That's right. I'd say I can get about ten others," answered Aaron. "Make it twenty," said Vicky seriously. "I'll get your job done...trust me," he said with a sneer. He turned and left the Valley.

The group began mumbling to each other and breaking up. "Wait, one more thing," boomed Oro, getting everyone's attention back. "I hope that none of you see any problems with my East side boys Nom and Mac joining the group, right?" He encountered no resistance. "It might also be a good idea if we meet somewhere later this week to discuss our next chance to steal the product. Anyone have a place?"

"Y'all can come back here. I can let you have the house to yourselves. James and I will be out anyway," offered Mr. Marah. "Appreciate it," said Oro. "Stan, can you contact your man in the Traditional ranks so he can come meet with us?" "Sure thing," he said. The group began to break off. When he reached the road, Oro turned to go with Nom. "I can't tell you how much I owe you, man. You saved not only my life, but the lives of seven other Urumqi." "That's what friends are for." As the seriousness gave in to the silliness, they both had a good laugh. "I gotta head home," said Oro, "but you be sure and keep me posted on your East side matters. I'll see you in a little bit."

Chapter Six-
Schemes

Ryan and Aan walked through the Great Circle. "My plan is working, wouldn't you say so Ryan?" "I guess so. I just don't see what we are gaining by arguing with the Big Man." Aan was ready for the question. "It is no longer arguing. Here's the way I see it. The Big Man knows that Dave's Agents are loyal to us. Before, most of the Agents in this area were at his disposal. He feels threatened by the loss, and now he knows that we know the full extent of our power. I doubt that he will quarrel with us again. And eventually, he may even beg us to help protect his products that are being stolen. Only then will we have full control of both the Agents and the Contemporaries." Ryan was satisfied with the answer. "So what should I tell the rest of the group?" he asked. "Well," said Aan, "tell them what they want to hear; it isn't so far from the truth. Tell them that we have successfully gained two powerful allies, the Agents and Contemporaries, and explain to them that the next step is to cleanse our Temple of those outcasts who move to stop us." Ryan looked worried. "Is this really what you plan to do?" "Certainly," said Aan, "Certainly."

Aaron Brown walked through the dusty streets of Imperial City[3]. He needed to speak with his client, because the deal that he had made with Oro Kanoka would slightly alter his plans. For years, he had served as the Empire's best mercenary. The reason he knew he was the best was because he always won. Now, he could no longer say that. His last two targets had been successfully protected by Kanoka and his other Urumqi. He knew that the Empire hated the Urumqi. He would need to think of a better excuse as to why his team of Mandos was nearly obliterated. As a

Mando, he rarely had other clients besides the Empire, so he would need to make his "new client" believable. He thought back as far as he could to the days when he used to play the field for clients. One in particular came to mind. The Big Man was his name. Since he was a shadowy, underworld-like figure, he would not likely be known by the Emperor. It was his only choice...

"Aaron, it is good to see you," nodded the old man in the direction of the doorway where the captain stood. "Sir," said Aaron respectfully. "Let's not deliberate," prompted the old man. "I must know: Was your party successful in destroying James Marah?" "No, sir." The old man's face fell, as if a decade of age had passed through his body in only a few seconds. The scar that ran the length of his face drooped even lower. "I am disappointed, Aaron. Never before have you failed me." The old man stood and limped slowly toward Aaron. The reason he limped was the loss of his right foot. In its place sat a metal crutch, fused right into his shin. "I must know, what is happening to you? You have failed two of the most important tasks set before you..." "I know that this will be difficult to hear, but I am no longer able to get by with such little pay and such weak comrades. I have been forced to rely on other clients to meet my needs." Aaron breathed a sigh of relief. He had done it.

"I'm confused. What other client is able to pay you more for his bounties than the Empire?" The old man was standing close to Aaron now. They studied each other, as if in a struggle of willpower. "I do not know his name; but in the underworld, he is known as the Big Man." "That is not a person I am familiar with..." The old man's voice was strong; a blind man would have thought him to be no older than forty. He reached up to rub his chin. Aaron saw the two fingers that were missing from his left hand. "You are my best fighter, Aaron. I will give you leave to take care of the 'Big Man' before I give you any further assignments.

Just promise me that if the Urumqi do surface, you will find yourself once again allied with us." "Yes, sir. Farewell."

The old man was a skeptic. 'Unless something good can be proven, it is in your best interest to assume the worst.' Those words had been passed down from Guranqi to Guranqi. And as the Guran[4], it was his job to follow them. The old man walked steadily down the hallway toward the Emperor's throne room. The limp was just an act. 'If an ally of yours thinks you are weak, he is likely to show his true colors.' The metal door that guarded the room kept out all but the most important allies of the Emperor. The old man slid it upward with a sweep of his hand. The Emperor was talking with his son. He waited for them to finish. "What is it, Guran?" "A pressing matter, sir: I have just spoken with Aaron Brown, the captain of your Mandos. He has informed me that he failed to terminate James Marah."

Viron stood. "What? Again? How can this be? Did he mention what the problem is? Does he need more men...more money?" asked the Emperor slowly. "Exactly, sir, but you know that I would not disturb you unless I have something useful to report. He says that he is unable to support himself by only working for us. He has mentioned...another client." "Who?" asked Viron coldly. "He does not know his name...an underworld figure to be precise, one known as the Big Man." Both men paused. "Does that name mean anything to you, sir?" asked the Guran. Viron dismissed the thought. "I know," spoke up the son. "Ha!" cackled the Guran. "Tell us." "During my infiltration of the Urumqi meetings, I have learned much about the other factions who are allied with the Urumqi. The Big Man is the leader of the Contemporaries and a close ally of Aan Huila's Urumqi. Also, I must add that a group of Agents are in on the deal. The Big Man serves as a median for the Agents to carry out the will of the Urumqi. This Big Man would be foolish to hire Aaron Brown as a client, while secretly working with Agents as well."

The two older men listened carefully. "The way I see it, there are three possible situations. One is that the Big Man is taking a gamble by using the Mandos to secretly do his bidding. If that is the case, then Aaron is probably still loyal to us. The other is that Aaron has been in contact with the Urumqi all along and is ready to leave the Empire and join the Urumqi. The third is that he is lying to us, using the Big Man as a decoy. After all, he could be caught up in the rift created by Kanoka. Viron nodded slowly. "Yes, my son, I now foresee that this is what Aaron has done. Guran, when Aaron returns to Imperial City, kill him." "It will be done, sir." The Guran left the room.

"Tell me, father, how is it that the Guran differs from yourself? Why don't you train the other Guranqi yourself?" "Any Guranqi that I would train would be likely to see my weaknesses and use them against me. With you, son, my trust in you is endless, as is your respect for me. With the Guran, my father was much more careful. He revealed his weakness, but used the trust that he placed in us to cover it up. Say that the Guran decided to overthrow me; he knows that your respect for me is strong enough to kill him if he were to kill me. That is why he knows his place. As for those that he trains, they have often tried to exploit his weaknesses, but they have all failed. It is not for no reason that he has that scar, you know."

Chapter Seven-
The Lovebirds

Oro was walking through the Great Circle to meet up with Vince and the others. He turned around quickly as he felt a hand on his shoulder. "Vicky told me about that kiss, Oro." It was Jordan. "Oh, hey," said Oro after a few seconds of silence. "You kinda snuck up on me there…" "Whatever," she interrupted. "So do you really like her? 'Cuz I know she's crazy about you. Want me to set you guys up? Ask her to come by your place today…" "Alright, Alright," interjected Oro as her words fell into place. "But wouldn't I be better off taking it slow?" She thought for a moment. "No, she might get bored." They both laughed. "So how about you and Stan? It seemed like you two were having a special moment together too…" "But I don't know if he likes me…" "Are you kidding me? Sure he does," clarified Vince, breaking up their private conversation. "Both of you need to make a move before it's too late." They gave Vince a skeptical look. "If you don't, I will do it for you," he laughed. "Whatever," said Jordan.

When they reached the center, everyone sat down without a word. "Well, are we all planning on just sitting and staring, or do we have something to talk about?" joked Jim. "Nah, I think we better give the lovebirds some time to themselves," answered Vince. "You told him!" shouted Vicky to Jordan, just as Stan was saying "We didn't do anything!" Silence. "You must have done something right," whispered Jordan as she slid her arm around Stan. Oro looked over at Vicky. "It's alright, no one's gonna find out…" She didn't say anything; her eyes showed her true feelings. Oro wasn't sure what to do. He followed Stan's lead and pulled her close to him. She placed her head on his shoulder. They just held each other for what seemed like an eternity until the clanging of the bell awakened them all to reality. "You all finished yet?" prompted Jim. "'Cuz I was hoping to find out when y'all were planning on meeting with the Mandos again." "Actually, my man says we have a job tomorrow night, so I was thinking today," said Stan. "Alright," nodded Vince. "Let's meet out front after class today to discuss the last minute stuff…"

Oro and Jim walked down the Technology hall. "Hey, is Dan going to be at our meeting today?" asked Oro. "Well he needs to be," said Jim, "so make sure he knows it's today." Jim went to his class, as did Oro. "Hey Dan, what's up?" called Oro when he saw his friend. "Oh, nothing much; still finding more uses for the blaster powder." "Well that's good, 'cuz we're gonna need some new technology for our assault on the Contemporaries tomorrow." Oro wondered just how much about the money Dan knew. Apparently enough, if he was expected at the meeting. "Actually, we're gonna meet today after school to discuss…" "Well," interjected Dan, "Am I invited to this one?" "Of course. Why? Have they failed to invite you in the past?" He paused. "I don't think that everyone accepts me as a part of the group," said Dan matter-of-factly. "Yeah, they don't exactly make it easy sometimes. I'm going through the same thing in a way; they don't really like my Urumqi buddies from the East side…"

Before they knew it, class was over. They walked out the gates to the old oak tree[5] where they had agreed to meet. The others were already there. Oro noticed the new boy, clearly a Traditional. "Yo Dan the man, what's goin on?" called out Vince cheerfully, drowning out the groans coming from Stan and Vicky. Oro liked how Vince had the ability to make other people feel welcome. Aan never had that. They set out for the Marah house. Oro caught up with Vince. Don't you think that Nom and Mac should be here to hear what we're planning?" Vince gave him a skeptical look.

"You know, I'm not so sure that everyone here trusts them. We're already taking a huge gamble by allowing Aaron's Mandos to help us. Involvement with the East side school could become a big conflict." "But we owe them all so much. They saved us from a deadly attack and you're giving Aaron more credit than them…"

"Fine," nodded Vince. "But I'm not sure how it's going to work out with the money situation. Assuming we can steal double or triple our usual amount, we would still receive the same cut and the rest will be needed to pay the Mandos…" "But without the East side Agents there, it is possible that the Mandos could show up with a greater force and kill us all." It was obvious that Vince had not thought about this. "Okay, how about this? They keep the product they steal and sell it themselves. That way, it makes things fair. After all, they still need our help to steal it." "Alright," said Oro, "but what about Nom and Mac? I need to pass along the information…" "No problem," said Vince. "Just be sure and keep it a secret from the others."

They climbed off of the road and into the small valley. The Marah house stood silent, its front porch crumbling away. Vicky led the group inside. The whole house looked dusty, almost uninhabited. Even the air had its own layers of dust that swirled to a halt when the company passed. No one used the furniture; they all sat down on the rug and waited. The new boy took a seat next to Oro. As the others found their places, Oro wondered if he should introduce himself. 'Why not go for it?' "Hey, I'm Oro," he said coolly. "I know," answered the boy. "Huh?" Oro was not expecting such an unconventional response. "Name's Nate Farelle, information dealer. I know who you are." Oro did not know what else to say.

"Alright, how about we pay attention," announced Vicky with fake sarcasm. "Here's the map we made up last time," she said, pulling the wrinkled piece of parchment out of her pocket. "What improvements have we got?" Vince spoke up. "Well, instead of using these single doors like last time, I think it's worth a shot trying to open this big door. Then we could get the boxes onto the carts twice as fast..." Vicky squeezed in between Oro and Nate, dropping the map in the center. She reached over to Oro and kissed him softly on the cheek. Oro saw that Jordan did the same to Stan. "Alright, it's not a contest everyone!" yelled Vince. "Go show off your kissing skills at home." "Oh, you bet we will, right Oro?" shot back Vicky. He didn't know what else to do besides nod, so that's what he did. "Wow, you people are strange," commented Nate after the short silence. "Look who's talking!" raved Jim. "You're the one who's stalking Oro. 'Heh, I know who you are, heh, I know where you live, heh.'" Everyone laughed.

"Alright, now how about we discuss the map," said Dan unexpectedly, causing everyone to look at him. Vince began, "Well, we need to figure out how to open that dock door. With all the help that we'll have, it would be much more efficient..." "What help?" interjected Nate. "Agents and Mandos mostly, and a few more Urumqi..." "You're being vague. I need more specific information..." "Give it a rest," said Vicky, elbowing Nate in the ribs. "You were saying, Vince..." "Yes, I think the Urumqi ought to go in first. We can confuse the guards, open the dock door, and let in Aaron's Mandos to lock down the place and help Nate's people with loading the product. Nate, will you have enough carts?" "Yes," he said tersely. "Now what about the Agents you mentioned? Or what about Dan, here?" he asked. Oro took the moment to answer Nate's questions. "Well, the Agents are managing their own products." "You mean you're letting them *have* product for free?" "We owe them a big favor. I would appreciate no further questions," commanded Oro with conviction.

As the meeting broke up, Jim caught up to Oro. "Way to go, man. That Nate has been on my nerves forever. I think you knocked some sense into him." Oro was pleased by the compliment. "And you kept Dan's technology away from him. That's one piece of information he won't have." "That's right. You know, I've been thinking...we have some serious allies now, and if tomorrow goes as planned, we may have a shot at reuniting the Urumqi..." "It's not going to happen," said Jim abruptly. "Why?" "People like Aan Huila don't deserve a second chance. He'll never change, never walk away."

As they reached the West Road, Vicky caught up with them. "Hey Oro, where you goin? You didn't forget about our date tonight did you?" He knew she was just playing, but that didn't make a response come any easier. "Aw I'm sorry girl, but I need to go catch up with Nom...you wanna come with me?" She shifted her playful smile. "Sure." They walked past the Crossroads[6] and followed the East Road to Nom's place. The house was alive with commotion as the huge family prepared the dinner. Nom's grandma answered the door. "Just a minute," she said warmly. When Nom came to the door, Oro introduced him to Vicky. "Hey there," said Nom cheerfully. "You owe this guy a lot for helping out your family. So therefore you owe me a lot too, 'cuz I saved this guy's life and then he saved yours." She wasn't sure what to say. "Well thanks," she mumbled. "C'mon, let's go take a walk; I have some things that I need to fill you in on."

They took to the old trail, where Oro explained the basics of the plans to Nom. "You've got yourself a deal," confirmed Nom. "Oh, by the way, what do you people call yourselves to distinguish you from Aan's people?" Oro looked at Vicky. "Well, we're the outcasts," he said slowly. "Then may the Few and True join the Outcasts!" "Few and True? Is that you and Mac?" "Yep...can't be late for dinner...I'll see you tomorrow."

"He's a funny little guy," commented Vicky on their journey back. "Yeah, he's the real deal. Hasn't hidden anything from me in thirteen years." As they passed by the Valley, Vicky stopped and looked at him. "Wanna stay with me tonight? I have the place all to myself you know..." "Sure." Normally, he would have thought about saying yes; but this time, he didn't. Nothing mattered besides her. 'The Urumqi might always be the underdogs in life, but I don't have to be. It's my time now. Besides, choice is an illusion...'

As Vicky bolted up the door for the night, Oro stacked a few logs into the fireplace. As he poured on the oil and opened the tinder box, Vicky was once again beside him. "You don't need that," she laughed, pulling out her staff. She touched it to the hearth and the fire sprang to life. "That's how we light fires in this family." The playful smile returned to her lips and the loving twinkle to her eyes. She wrestled him to the floor, pinning his arms with her elbows. They kissed. "Well, are you ready?" Time stopped. Oro saw Aan's smirking face. 'What are you going to do, Oro? You can't do it, can you? You're too weak...' "More than ready," he answered as *his* playful smile returned to his lips.

Chapter Eight- The Coast

Ryan Rider stood atop the chest at the end of the corridor at the back of the Great Circle. "It is with great pride that I tell you all that I believe I have finally discovered our purpose." The room grew silent. "When our parents told us of the Urumqi, their message was to find others like us. In the beginning, we took our meeting place for granted. In reality, that was the challenge! We have successfully separated the true from the untrue. I believe that it will soon be time to close the gap. We must destroy those who we have left behind!" Aan encouraged the less sure Urumqi by clapping loudly. He was soon joined by Slay and Zach, and then by all except for Seth and Ja. They stood in the back, whispering to each other. "What's gotten into him?" asked Seth. "I mean I know he's a little off sometimes, but he's acting like the Urumqi could be his elite killing machine…" "I don't know," said Ja irritably, hoping that Seth would just be quiet.

In reality, Ja did know. As he moved away to the corner of the room, he thought. He thought about the Emperor's decree that had split so many friends and families apart. He thought about Nom, a friend he would likely never see again. He thought about Oro, knew that he saw the problems festering within this room. He thought of Aan's anger as he threatened Jim, and later Oro. Aan was the reason that everyone was angry and afraid and hurt. 'But problems best not be solved,' he thought. 'If I confront him, it will hurt me more…'

Ryan continued. "Now that we have strong alliances with both the Agents and the Contemporaries, I feel that we have a good chance of carrying out this task we have set before ourselves…" "Speaking of such," interrupted Wanda, "we should also discuss the problem that one of our allies is facing. The Big Man needs help defending his product out near the coast. I suggest that we send a small group to figure out what is happening down there…" Aan smiled, knowing that he had told her to say this. "I will go," he called out. His enthusiasm caused Slay to yell out the same. "I'm with you, buddy," called Zach. "It is settled then," boomed Wanda. "The three of you will go down to the warehouse tonight and help our allies."

When Oro awoke the next morning, he found himself curled beside Vicky on the old couch by the fire. A few embers were still aglow in the hearth. He turned his head and kissed her softly. "Hey," she said quietly. She didn't waste much time in getting up. Throwing on some fresh clothes, she went to the kitchen and salvaged breakfast from the pantry. Oro soon joined her and they ate in silence. Oro stared out the back window and saw for the first time the Valley beyond. The sun was already high in the sky. "We're already late for school, huh?" "Yeah." She seemed entirely unfazed by this. They tossed their bowls onto the counter and headed out.

At the Great Circle, the guards demanded to see their schedules as usual. Both were marked with a red X in the corner. "If you're late again, we'll know about it," sneered the guard as he gave back Oro's schedule. No one was wandering inside the Circle; everyone was in class. "I'll see you in a bit," mumbled Oro as he headed for Math.

"Why are you so late?" bellowed the beefy instructor. Oro was tired; he didn't feel like arguing. He pulled out his staff and pointed it at the instructor. "You don't care why I'm late. Go back to your lesson." He said nothing. The rest of the class gawked at him. As Oro sat down, he thought about how stupid he had been to show an Imperial instructor that he was an Urumqi. But his will was stronger; the instructor would never remember the encounter with Oro Kanoka.

Lunch seemed to come later than usual. As Oro trudged through the mess of students, he saw that the others were already there. Even Dan had felt the need to come by. "Alright, let's go over the plans one more time," prompted Vince. "First off, all of us need to bring our staffs and our blasters. Dan, if it isn't a problem, please bring as many extra blasters as you can..." "I haven't finished working with the technology yet. No one else should be allowed to use..." "Dan!" interjected Jim, "we're going to need them. I'm sure no one will steal them." It was obvious that Dan was still skeptical. "Okay."

"Anyway," continued Vince, "do the Mandos and Agents know where to go and when to come?" Stan answered, "My people have been in touch with Aaron. He knows where to go and will arrive there with his people at the same time as us, as will the Traditionals." "According to Nom, he and Mac are going with the Agents ahead of time to check out the area," offered Oro. "They won't act until all of us arrive..." "Great," finished Vince. "And they know to bring their own carts?" "Yep." Silence. "One more thing," prompted Stan. After class, we are going to meet at the Crossroads, and then walk up to my place where we can ride with Nate to the coast instead of walking all that way." "Sounds good," said Vince.

During technology, Dan was not as quiet as usual. "My family knows about the blaster powder now," he said, as they broached the subject of weapons. "They don't quite understand it though." "What do you mean?" asked Oro. Dan hesitated. "They don't understand how big and important of a discovery it is. They want to just start selling it off. They don't realize that pretty soon, someone is going to break open a capsule and discover the mystery of what's inside. They don't know what they're doing..." "I'm sorry to hear that, man," said Oro seriously. "Not to change the subject, but what do you plan on doing tonight? Are you just going to sit back and wait while the others do the work?" "No, I'm gonna help out too so I can keep an eye on whoever's using my blasters." "Smart," said Oro, for lack of another word. "Are you riding with us to the coast?" "Yeah, I've gotta run home first for the stuff though, so tell them to wait up for me."

After class, Oro met up with Vicky and they began the walk to Stan's. "I don't trust the Mandos," declared Vicky, breaking the silence. "Why not?" "Do I need a reason? They're Mandos, that's why." Oro wasn't sure if now was the time to tell her what he thought. "It's not just the Mandos, is it? You don't trust my friends either." "Do I have a reason to trust them?" "No, but you don't have a reason to distrust them. Why assume the worst?" "False trust is worse than no trust at all," she said, clearly meaning to end the conversation. "That's not true. You can't go living life angry just because there are a few rotten people out there. Just because I had false trust in Aan doesn't mean I won't trust anyone because of that." Oro knew he hit home, but he saw that she refused to let it show.

Stan's place was in the midst of a jumble of little homes and buildings centered on the flats off of the East Road. Oro was surprised to see people about, some hanging clothes out to dry, others tending small gardens. It was clearly a Traditional community. "There it is," said Vicky pointing. The otherwise inconspicuous house was glorified by the entourage of vehicles lined up on its drive. Oro saw Nate Farelle and about thirty other Traditionals tending the mules and checking the carts for potential problem areas. Since he and Vicky had taken their time, the others were already there, except for Dan, of course. "Yo, Oro," called out Vince. "Hop on, let's get going." "Not yet," he yelled back, "we're still waiting for Dan." "Are you kidding? With all the money we give him, he can't even get his own ride?"

asked Vicky. "Give it a rest," said Oro irritably. "We need his help." He looked Vicky in the eye. She looked away.

Dan soon came, bearing five blasters, and the group took off down the road. Each cart was given a bit of a head start, as not to arouse suspicion. Oro, Vicky, Vince, and Dan rode aboard the last, driven by Nate. As they bounced along the gravel road, Dan asked "Who's going to be getting these, anyway?" Before Vince could answer, Oro said "Nom and Mac need them most. And Max Toko ought to have one as well. That's three." "That leaves two for Aaron's group," finished Vince. Satisfied with the answer, but still rather unsure, Dan kept quiet for the rest of the trip.

A few minutes beyond the Crossroads, the landscape began to change. Homes gave way to plazas and marketplaces, where the Contemporaries made, as well as spent, most of their money. Beyond that were the factories and lumber mills that produced the goods sold in the City and beyond that was the coast itself. Although Oro had never seen the ocean before, he was rather disappointed. As a child, he remembered Yia's stories of the beauty of the waves. Now all he saw was the filth that the water had been forced to consume. Their destination was the old dock across from the Big Man's warehouse. Now that the marketplaces were far from the water, the boats that once populated the harbor were nowhere to be seen. Nom and the others were nowhere in sight. As Nate directed the others, Oro explored the immediate area. As he slid down the hill to the beachfront, he heard a voice call out. "Who goes there?" "It's me, Max," answered Oro. The not so small group of about thirty Agents had set up camp under the wreckage of the docks. "Where's Nom?" "He's with Mac around the far side of the building. They're watching the carts for us." "Why don't you all go check in with Vince. He'll fill you guys in on the plans."

Oro climbed quickly back up the rocks to the far side of the warehouse. He motioned for Nom and Mac to follow; they acknowledged without a word. The entire group assembled quickly around Vince. "Okay, let's go over our plan. When Aaron arrives, we'll begin. Dan, you take care of handing out the blasters. Urumqi, we will go in first. Stan and Jim take the back; Vicky and Jordan, side, and the four of us will go in the front. Once we're all in, meet at the dock door. You too, Dan, 'cuz we may need some help with the lock. When we get the big door open, Agents and Traditionals begin loading your carts. When you hear my word, drop everything and leave. Now when Aaron gets here…" "Yes," said the cold voice behind Vince. "Oh, hey. Kinda snuck up on me there…anyway, listen to Nate and help his men load the boxes. Let's go!"

"One-two-three!" counted Vince, and with Oro's help, he kicked open the front door. Prior to the invasion, the guards sat smoking. "Hey!" shouted the closest one, but it was too late. Vince grabbed him and threw him to the ground. "You will stay there and be quiet," said Vince, pointing his staff. Two more guards came, but the Urumqi were too fast. Nom used the same tactic on them, leaving all of them there in the entryway. "Could one of you stay here and keep watch?" asked Vince. "Sure," said Mac. All the doors had one guard each. Jim stood watch at the back, as did Jordan at the side. The five remaining Urumqi, with Dan tagging along beside them, met at the dock door. "It's only held shut here at the bottom," announced Dan. "Just gotta undo this chain and…" Stan was way ahead of him. He quickly picked the lock, which was one of his many unique talents. "Okay, let's concentrate and lift it," suggested Oro. The door did not budge. "Hold on, I think there's a bracket holding it down from the top," said Dan. Nom waved his hand; the bracket fell clumsily to the ground. "Nice touch," noted Stan.

Chapter Nine-
Minor Confrontations

Aaron watched from the outside as the door slid open. He hooked one of the blasters onto his equipment pack and handed the other one to one of his colleagues. He had to admit that the concept was unique. No other Mando could say that he had used a fire-powered weapon. Loading the boxes soon became boring, so he started looking around. The warehouse was too big to see wall to wall; it made him feel as though someone could be watching...

Nate stood at the big door, so that he had a clear view of both the inside and the outside. There was too much information to keep straight. In his opinion, he was loosing ground. The Agents, Mandos, and Urumqi could potentially steal the product by themselves. 'It won't be long until they get rid of me,' he thought. He quickly turned his head to look down an empty aisle; something, or someone, had caught his eye. "Hey, come with me," he called to one of his men. He eased slowly down the aisle. Boxes gave way to burlap sacks filled with fruits and herbs. He pulled out a decent sized dagger as he made his way down a row of potatoes. The blow to the head gave him no time to call out for help. "What the..." yelled the other Traditional before Aan Huila struck him down.

"Get out! GET OUT!" bellowed Vince. The Agents were quick to retreat with their bounty, not waiting for Nom or Mac. The Traditionals scrambled to their carts, waiting for their leader, who would never come. Aaron ran to the place he heard the yell. When he saw three unknown Urumqi with their staffs drawn, he made a quick decision. Pulling out his tinderbox, he ignited his blaster and fired it straight at Aan, giving his gang some time to regroup. Aan dodged the shot neatly, ran down a side aisle, and came face to face with Nom Patal. "Hello old friend," said Aan weakly. "I would have thought better of you. Urumqi shouldn't resort to stealing; you're better than that…" "I know what you did, Aan. You have betrayed the Urumqi." The smile vanished from Aan's face. "Step aside, Nom. You can't beat me." "No!" Nom gathered all the force that he could and threw Aan back with a sweep of his staff.

Not more than two aisles down, Oro had found Slay Ander. Like true enemies, they exchanged no words, only blows. As Aaron ran for the dock door, Zach Johnson leapt out at him, dealing a heavy blow to his chest. Aaron fell back in pain, but soon recovered, due to the chain mail that lined his body. He slashed away with his scimitar in time to block Zach's next blow. Pushing his staff aside, Aaron grabbed the small Urumqi by the neck and swept his legs out from under him with a roundhouse kick. With amazing strength, he hoisted Zach above his head and threw him into the rows of potatoes, where he collided with Aan and Slay. Without thinking, Aaron threw a cable around one of the colossal makeshift-shelving units and crashed it down upon the three Urumqi. "LET'S GO!" he called to his men.

Dan scrambled about, trying to recover his five blasters. He easily found the one that Max had dropped. Aaron's was stumbled upon by Stan, who tossed it over to Dan as they headed for the carts. Nom and Mac had held onto theirs and returned them to Dan as planned. One was missing. "We gotta go!" yelled Oro, pulling Dan toward the door. Vince had found Nate's body, and tried to explain to the other Traditionals that their leader was dead. With Stan's urging, the Traditional carts wasted little time in fleeing the coast with their product, leaving no one behind.

The Traditional carts followed the setting sun toward Stan's place. When they arrived, the little town lay silent. Vince muttered apologies to a few of the drivers for the loss of their leader. Stan spoke with another Traditional boy, making the arrangements to receive their cut of the cash. Dan was clearly upset by the loss of the blaster that he had been forced to leave behind. Jordan tried her best to tell him it was okay. Nom and Mac did not linger long, each setting out for home.

Oro knew that he needed to get home as well. It dawned on him that his parents had no idea where he was last night and that they would be furious with him. He needed to stop by Yia's to see if she could cover for him. As he turned to leave, Vicky gave him a quick kiss. "See you later," he said under his breath.

Sitting with Yia on her front porch, Oro wasted little time in telling her about his adventure with the Traditionals. He left out the part about Vicky, saying that he couldn't come home because they had to plan the attack. He wasn't sure if he was ready to tell her yet. Without even asking, she offered to walk home with him and try to explain everything to his parents.

"I cannot believe how irresponsible you were," said Steve Kanoka[7] once he was alone with Oro. "It was ridiculous of you to think that spending the night with your friends without telling me is acceptable. I don't care if Yia says you had to. She has no way of justifying herself. The Urumqi are a bad influence on you." He paused to catch his breath. Oro took the opportunity to get in his last word. "Why did you abandon the Urumqi? What is it that Yia has that you don't?" Silence. "I can't tell you that, son..." "See, you don't have a reason either. And no one makes you feel bad about your choice!"

"Father, I have good news." Viron's son stood in the doorway of the throne room, looking up at the Emperor. "Yes." "I have discovered exactly who is allied with

Kanoka's Urumqi. At the coast, Agents, Traditionals, and Mandos helped Kanoka steal whatever it is that they wanted. The Agents were led by Max Toko, a smalltime captain from East side school. The Traditionals were those closest to Nate Farelle, another smalltime character who didn't survive the assault. As for the Mandos, we were right; Aaron Brown and about twenty others are working for Kanoka." "Good," cackled Viron slowly. "The final steps in our plan will soon be a reality. Kanoka and Huila will fight to the death and there will be none left to oppose us." The son lingered. "More to say?" asked the father. "What of the chest? Don't the Urumqi still have its power?" Viron smiled. "The chest that you speak of has been taken care of. Theirs is but an icon for hope. Nonetheless, raping them of the chest would be a critical blow." "It will be done, father."

Aan stood gloomily against the wall in the History hall. He hoped that Ryan would show up soon; he was tired of sloughing off the dirty looks that the passersby shot at him. The defeat that his small group had suffered was still fresh in his mind, as was his encounter with a stern-faced Nom, who had shown no signs of taking his side. Ryan plowed through the double doors, knocking those smaller than him aside with his every step. "Well...how did it go?" he asked enthusiastically, choosing not to comprehend the answer written across Aan's face. "Not good, my friend." Before Ryan could respond, Aan blurted, "Nom Patal and another East side boy have joined up with Oro. He also had help from an organized group of Traditionals and nearly thirty Agents in league with Max Toko!" Ryan had no idea what to say, so he kept quiet. "And most disturbing of all, he now seems to be on good terms with the Mandos' captain."

"So..." inquired Ryan nervously. "We must go ahead with my plan sooner than expected," breathed Aan. "Can we? I mean, realistically, do we still have enough assets to guarantee us a victory?" For the first time ever, Aan looked Ryan in the eye. "We still have three more Urumqi than they do. Dave's group is roughly forty strong. As for the Big Man, we must request that he lend us all of his guards…anyway, it seems that the odds are evenly stacked." Ryan seemed satisfied with that answer. "But what about..." "It will be safe, I assure you," broke in Aan.

Oro's day began just as gloomily as Aan's. His parents' mood had not improved much, which made his home life harder. After passing through the gate, he snatched his schedule back from the guard only to notice the red X. He thought about his night with Vicky. But then he remembered Jade.

At lunchtime, the group converged at the center. Everyone was in a rather dark mood except for Stan, who pulled out several neatly bundled roles of coins. "They paid us already?" asked Jordan hopefully. "Yeah," beamed Stan. "I got it all figured out with the Main Man..." "The who?" asked Jim. "I don't know his name," said Stan, "he's taken over for Nate I guess. I call him the Main Man." "Whatever," said Jim, but he couldn't help but chuckle.

"Sorry to interrupt the giggles, but there's something I need to tell you." Vince had succeeded in completely removing expression from his face. His flat tone caused the others to pay attention. He pulled out a piece of parchment from his coat pocket and unfolded it slowly. "Here's what this says. 'Aan: I will be anxious to hear from you tomorrow so that you can report your findings from the coast. Regardless of Oro's involvement, there is one thing that still concerns me. The chest that sits in the middle of our meeting room is an heirloom of the Urumqi. I am told that it gives us great power. We must be extra careful now that our enemies have grown powerful. Without this chest, our cause may be forever lost. Ryan'" "Where'd you find that?" exclaimed Oro. Vince was quiet, as if in deep thought. "I found it next to Nate's body," he spat quickly. "And…" prompted Jim.

"This is it," said Vince coolly. "If we can steal this chest, their willpower will be broken."

The clanging of the bell was almost welcomed; the six outcasts split up to go to their classes. "Why do you think he waited until now to tell us?" mused Jim as he walked with Oro to technology. "I don't know, man. It does seem odd though, especially for Vince. I'd have thought he'd have been all over it with us on the ride home." To Oro, time stood still. He was only half heartedly listening to Dan's whining about the lost blaster. 'Why would Aan leave something so important behind? Why was it that Vince happened to find the note? Why did Ryan specify the importance of the chest and not the importance of the stolen product? Could Vince have forged the note? Why would he be so determined to steal the chest?' He remembered as far back as he could to his first day with the Urumqi. He remembered Ryan's words. 'Viron's spies can get through the door. They did it once, they can do it again.' Then there was Yia's advice. 'Only the Guranqi know where you meet.' But Vince was the only person who saw the same faults in the Urumqi as he did. It was crazy to assume that Vince was a spy just because of a few unanswered questions.

Jade Hira sat alone in the room that used to belong to her parents. She had never wanted to go through her parents' things; now her curiosity had gotten the better of her. She opened the first chest and found a small collection of very old books. She picked up one of the bigger ones and opened up to somewhere in the middle. The words were neatly centered, although clearly written by hand. *It's hard to walk this path alone; hard to know which way to go. Will I ever save this day? Will they ever change?*

'Only bad people leave the Urumqi.' Surely that couldn't be true. Reading the words on the page, she thought about Oro. 'He would have liked this song,' she thought. *Will they open their eyes, and realize we are one? On and on we stand alone until our day is done. Will they open their eyes, and realize we are One...* She thought about what Oro had said. 'Well that's why they're dead now. Shows you how much they knew.' She had said those words to herself many times; she decided that this would be the last. Jade Hira would open her eyes; she would forgive Oro Kanoka.

Chapter Ten- Impending Fear

Time went by as slowly as ever in the lands of Uru. Wanda Mardi and Ryan Ridder talked themselves insane, persuading the Urumqi that it was time to wipe out the 'Outcasts'. Aan Huila fretted over something of relative importance. Ja Kahn felt more alone than ever. Seth was simply confused. Nom Patal sat with his grandmother, learning how to further control his willpower. Jim was letting Stan in on his doubts about Vince. Oro spent his day thinking of reasons not to head home after school. Vicky was the same as always, although after their disagreement over Oro's East side friends, she never wanted to 'talk.' And unknown to any other in Uru, Yia Kanoka cracked the lock on the old curio cabinet with a flick of her hand; she felt as though she might soon need her staff…

The day finally came when the waves of tension that pulsated through the Urumqi of West side school would be lifted. "We can't keep idling!" blurted Vince, causing Vicky to pull suddenly away from Oro. "I say we stop this nonsense! Tonight is the night. Oro, I know you can get your East side people, right? And Stan's already paid Aaron, so we have his team, plus the Main Man could spare a few people if he knew it was a free shot at the Big Man…" "I don't know…" breathed Stan slowly. "Let's just get it done," interrupted Jordan. "We all hate just sitting here. Why not give it a go and be done with all this?" There was no turning back now; everyone knew Jordan was right. "So we're all in?" asked Vince with renewed vigor. Oro was by far the least enthusiastic, but he didn't let it show.

In technology, Oro told Dan about the chest, and how Vince was determined to get it. "You know what? This is all crazy," interrupted Dan before Oro could finish. "You don't really expect me to lend you more of my technology just to have it stolen, do you? You all don't even consider me a part of your group and I'm tired of doing favors when I don't receive any in return." He looked away. "Sorry, Oro."

After class, Oro met up with the others one last time. "We're all going to meet back here at dusk tonight, right?" asked Vince for the tenth time. "Right…" mumbled Oro. As they split up, Vicky cornered him with a playful push. "Where do you think you're going?" "Sorry, I have to go by Nom's place to work out a few things with him." "I can't tag along this time?" "I'd rather you didn't; I'm not sure that he trusts you." Even though Oro was serious, Vicky thought he was just teasing her. She threw her arms around his shoulders and they kissed. 'It might be the last time,' thought Oro.

"Sup man, I figured I'd hear from you," called out Nom cheerfully as soon as he saw Oro. Nom kept the small talk to a minimum as Oro retold Vince's findings of Aan's note. "Aan never loses things," said Nom abruptly. "I know," breathed Oro. "But even if Vince isn't who he claims to be, I think we still have them outgunned." "What do you mean?" asked Nom. "Look, we need Max's Agents to help combat Aan. If we win, we grab the chest and get the heck away before Vince can do a single thing. Stan's already given me the money to hire them up front. We could give it a shot." Nom was deep in thought. Taking a gamble was not something that the Urumqi were known for. After a long silence, he grinned. "Right."

They set out toward Max's place, Nom leading the way. "Yo Max, quick job for you here," inquired Nom. "Not really quick," mumbled Oro. "We need as many people as you have tonight. I have the money up front." Suspecting a trick, Max asked "Why? Who are we fighting?" "Dave Datsun," said Nom with conviction before Oro could answer. "Really…" mused Max. "Forget about the cash for now; I'll need to start getting my team together. What time and where?" "At the West side school at dusk," called out Oro, for he and Nom had already set out from the house.

"Why'd you tell him about Dave?" asked Oro once they were out of earshot. "Because he needed a reason to try his hardest; he never forgot how Dave left him, judged him as unworthy to be an Agent." They were headed for Mac's place, their last stop before returning to West side school to face the challenge that awaited them.

"You are sure tonight is the night?" asked Ryan as he walked the West Road with Aan. "Yes, I am sure it is tonight." "Not to disagree, but how can you be sure?" asked Ryan skeptically. "There is one in their midst who is not an Urumqi." "A spy?" "No, just a friend. I first heard his name spoken when I saw him at the coast; he is a tech called Dan Carver. Since then, I have been able to know much of what he knows. Oro told him everything today. And if that is not reason enough, Derek is sure of it." "Since when do you listen to Derek?" "I don't." spat Aan. "But it seems to me that because he has no staff, no will to fight, he is more skilled in perception." "Whatever," grumbled Ryan. "Let's meet up back at the school as soon as we can. We'll need to organize everyone and such…"

Aan used his time window to go see Wendy. He felt that lately he had taken her for granted and he wanted to make sure that she felt a part of things. "Hey babe," he whispered, as he pulled her close to him. They too shared what could have been their last kiss.

Slay was first to arrive back at West side school. Only a few guards remained. He wasted no time in killing them with sharp blows to the head. Seth was next to arrive. With a sweep of his hand, he cracked open the locks that pinned the gates closed. When Wanda showed up, she forced her way into each of the hallways around the Circle, designating the left side for Dave's Agents and the right for the Big Man's guards, whom Ryan had insisted upon borrowing.

Aan made it inside the Circle before nightfall. Little did he know that Oro's group was already assembling in the gully on the side of the road. When he entered the Circle, he was pleased to see that Dave's group was indeed forty strong, and that Ryan had mustered quite a force of Contemporary guards just incase. "Do I dare ask if everyone is here?" joked Wanda once the entire legion was in order. "No, Ja isn't here," answered Aan. "But he's always late. I still think we're forgetting someone though." Time passed slowly to those waiting in the crammed hallways. "Where's Derek?" blurted Slay, after what seemed like forever. "Blast, I can't believe he ditched us," fumed Ryan angrily. "I was right," noted Aan. "Guess he knows he isn't much of a fighter."

"Well, are we all set?" asked Vince. This time there was finality in his voice. "Main Man?" "Yep, we ready." "Aaron?" "More than ever." "Max?" "All good down here, man." "Okay, Urumqi first, then Agents and Mandos, followed up by the rest. Let's go!"

Chapter Eleven- Major Confrontations

Oro was surprised to see the gates wrenched open. The full moon gave them an eerie glow at most, not enough to see what lay beyond. The eight Urumqi made their way into the Great Circle. "Shh, what's that noise?" whispered Oro, elbowing Nom in the shoulder. A faint splashing could barely be heard, just behind where they stood. Without warning, the entryway burst forth in flames. The entire Circle was bathed in light; Aan Huila stood in front of them laughing. "Aren't you a little outnumbered, Oro?" "I don't think so, Aan. Numbers mean nothing. My will is stronger than yours." In one quick motion, Oro tore Aan off his feet, ripping his brown jacket in the process. "Kill them!" shouted Aan. The corridors burst to life as hundreds of Agents and Contemporaries poured out of their hiding places. "Max! Lead the others to the outer doors!" called Nom through the blaze. "I got it!" blurted Stan. He raced down the nearest hallway, knocking aside Agents by spinning his staff. At the far door, he forced the lock open with a sweep of his hand. The Main Man rushed in, grabbing a bent sword left behind by an Agent that Stan had killed.

When it came down to working for the money, Aaron Brown was a loner. He saw no reason to wait for the doors to open. He threw a cable with a triple anchor on top of the roof of the nearest cluster of classrooms, and quickly scaled the wall. He left a few more anchors for the rest of his men to follow. Upon reaching the top, he spotted the man he was looking for. The Urumqi were being pushed back by the combination of Aan's attacks and the overwhelming number of Contemporaries and Agents that had yet to be neutralized by Max and Aaron. Zach Johnson was helping Slay flank Mac Kalomo against the fire that blocked the front gate. Aaron jumped awkwardly from the roof and landed with a thud between Mac and the flames. He whipped out his scimitar and lunged at Zach, knocking him away from the brawl. His push was countered by a quick swipe to the foot, causing him to fall backward. Zach used the opportunity to kick Aaron, meanwhile forcing his staff downward toward his throat.

Stan cut across the fray to the left, having opened all possible doors on the right. At the end of the Tech hall, the door did not open. He jabbed at it with his staff; nothing happened. "You cannot hide from me," cackled the thin figure clad in a tattered brown robe. Ja Kahn moved so quickly that one may have thought he appeared out of nowhere. He seized Stan's staff and jumped away, pulling himself through an air vent in the ceiling. Stan followed, angry that he had been so easily caught off guard. Ja soon reached the rooftop where he crouched behind the duct, knowing that Stan would follow. Before Ja could strike, Stan jumped from the opening and ripped away his staff. "Ha. This is only the beginning," warned Ja as he inched closer to Stan.

Jim's style was offense, not defense. Although he had taken a good number of blows, those that he dealt were much more effective. Cutting through the line of Urumqi, he made it to the back of the Circle. It almost seemed too easy. As he reached out for the door, Seth Andora forced him back with a flurry of blows. In his anger, Seth tore off the metal door of the secret hall, which Jim picked up and used as a weapon, manipulating it to slam into Seth from behind. With little time in between, Seth used the same strategy with any loose objects he could find. Soon the wall stones became the weapon of choice, flying great distances mostly to be blocked by a simple sweep of a staff.

Nom Patal knew that he was well trained. Deciding who he should choose to duel could make the difference between victory and defeat. He knew that Oro needed to settle the score with Aan, and Vince was doing okay against Ryan. Out of the corner of his eye, he saw Wanda Mardi's staff begin to turn blue. Before she could use her energy, he threw his staff, which knocked her down for a quick moment. He rushed up to her and plunged down for his staff, recovering it neatly with a rolling dodge. Their blows were so quick that a passerby would have yet to see them. Wanda had the advantage of a bit longer staff, but Nom's defensive jumps and dodges balanced things out.

"I hate you. I hate you!" shouted Vince as he squelched Ryan's blows with a powerful combo of his own. Ryan's style was too clean cut to defend against Vince entirely. Vince used his momentum advantage to knock Ryan back with a lateral blow whenever he got too close. About to be cornered against the wall, Ryan let go of his staff with one hand and reached for Vince's knee. With unexpected strength, he pulled Vince off balance and he crashed to the floor. From then on it was less of a duel and more of a sabotage as Ryan continuously dealt heavy blows to Vince, leaving no time for him to get up. However, Vince was far from giving up.

With a quick boost from Dave, the thin boy grabbed onto the edge of an air duct and pulled himself up onto the roof. Pulling out his bow, he began to pick off targets in the courtyard below. In the midst of his speed-duel with Ja, Stan saw an arrow strike Jordan in the forearm. In a torrent of rage, he leapt at the thin boy, kicking him off the edge. Ja used the almost perfect opportunity to deliver a spinning kick to Stan's head, knocking him off of the rooftop as well.

Below, Dave Datsun peered around the corner, sword in hand. He knew that Max Toko would look for him; they had been apart for far too long. However, this time, things would be different. Dave forced himself to forget the friendship and the good times that he once had with Max. He saw his enemy round the corner. At first, he wondered how to proceed, but the thought soon passed. He leapt out at Max, sword slashing wildly, catching the other Agent by surprise. "You shouldn't have come back," growled Dave warningly. "Leave now and you will live to be rich…" Max just smiled. "No, old friend. It isn't about the money. It's the thrill that keeps me going." Pulling a second sword from his equipment pack, Max continued the rampage with double the swords as Dave.

In the heart of the Great Circle, Vicky and Jordan were left to face the four remaining Urumqi, consisting of Ava, Mandi, Wendy, and Shelly. Although outnumbered, Jordan's unique fighting style involving two staffs was ideal for fighting multiple adversaries, as was Vicky's extra long weapon, which could deal a powerful blow from the front, or behind. Consequently, Ava's goal was to push her attackers back so that her three allies could press a forward attack as opposed to dodging the random blows from anywhere else.

"Look around, Oro. You have no chance. My fighters are better than yours. Even if your skills are as powerful as you boast, you will not have the chest!" Although the others were quick to fight, Oro and Aan just stood, circling each other. "You're all talk, Aan. You're just afraid that I might knock you down and embarrass you, so you're waiting for your precious Ryan to come and help you." The color drained from Aan's face. No one had ever called him an outright coward. He lunged at Oro, sweeping him aside with a wave of his staff without even touching him. Oro recovered with a forward roll, flipping himself upright close to his enemy, where he got in a quick blow before Aan could think defense. Oro's second strike resulted in a lock, which produced an earsplitting metal-on-metal sound, brought to life by the blue sparks that jumped across their staffs.

Lightning cracked across the sky; the rain wasted no time in following. Dan Carver lay in bed, feeling guilty about not helping his friend. He then reminded himself of all the times when he had gone out of his way to help somebody, only to get thrown down, not the least of which was Vince's request to use the blasters during the coast raid. But then he thought about the future. 'Surely Oro must have been disappointed when he found out that Aan hated him. But did that stop him from trusting me? No.' Dan knew what he had to do. Little did he know that there was another in Uru thinking those very same thoughts about Oro as he was.

Aaron couldn't hold back Zach's staff for much longer. His other hand groped through his equipment pack in the hopes of finding something useful. A spool of razor wire, spiked knuckles, knives, daggers... With a desperate throw, he looped the wire around Zach's foot and pulled. He fell off balance, leaving Aaron more than enough time to touch the scimitar to his throat.

Ja did not hesitate; with unnatural speed, he flipped himself off of the rooftop and attacked with several quick midair blows before Stan had any time to recover. With a well timed flip kick, Stan Mitchel knocked Ja away from him, and rushed him with a deadly whirling of his staff. Ja was much too fast. An easy shunt, combined with a rolling dodge, brought him straight behind Stan, where he delivered his final blow across Stan's back. "It's over," Ja whispered.

Tired of hurling the bricks, Jim Lars rushed at Seth, staff glowing blue with anger. Seth flipped his staff into his left hand, causing Jim to prepare for a two-strike blow on the right. He veered left to avoid it. Seth's trap had worked; his kick knocked Jim to the ground and his left handed follow-up ensured that he would stay down.

'She's getting too angry,' thought Nom. In between the attacks she was blocking, Wanda's weapon took on that eerie shade of blue as she tried to blast Nom with her power. So far, he had succeeded in forcing her to block before she could get off her attack, but time was running out. Nom stood still for not a second too long; Wanda's staff crackled as the blue electric shot toward Nom. He jumped high in the air, landing squarely behind her. He shot his hand forward, forcing his enemy's staff to come flying into his hand. Using a spin kick, he dashed her chances of winning.

Mac and Slay were deadlocked near the front of the courtyard, each struggling to push away the others' weapon. With renewed strength, Slay forced Mac to stumble backwards toward the fire. Mac rolled sideways to avoid the flames, but it was too late. Slay threw a punch that exploded against Mac, causing him to yell as the blue electric crackled about his body.

Stuck between the wall and four dangerous Urumqi, Vicky was feeling a bit worried. 'What would my dad do?' she thought. She remembered the day they fought the Mandos, as if it were so long ago. 'He would have killed Aaron,' she remembered. She knew she had to try harder. Usually alternating attacks, Wendy and Shelly were also eager to finish things up. They both rushed in at once, trying to overwhelm Vicky with a flurry of quick blows. Vicky knew this was her only chance. She turned her staff sideways and rammed her attackers with a lateral blow. Knocking both of them off their feet, she flipped her staff around and plunged it down at Shelly. "No!" yelled Wendy. Vicky slowly pulled the bloody end of her staff away. Shelly laid there motionless.

Vince lay on the ground, taking the beating from Ryan. His grip on his staff began to loosen. With a powerful blow, Ryan knocked it loose. "I win," breathed Ryan, pointing the edge of his staff toward Vince's throat. "No," said Vince calmly. He raised his hands; light cracked from the tips of his fingers, hurling Ryan across the courtyard. Vince ran for the metal doors, breaking the remaining one open by sweeping his hand.

Aan won the shunt, following it up with a series of attacks that forced Oro to fall back. Using his weight advantage, Aan continuously forced Oro backward until there was no place to go. "I told you; you can't win," sneered Aan, as he lowered his staff awaiting a comeback. Oro lunged out with his left hand and held fast to Aan's staff. Frustrated, Aan tried franticly to knock Oro away. With a sweep of his other hand, Oro pushed with all his power; Aan jerked backward, his staff snapping in two. He had done it! Aan staggered to a halt at the back of the Circle just in time to see Vince running down the corridor. He threw the remaining piece of his staff, striking Vince in the shoulder. This was all he had time for before Oro lifted him into the air. "Give me one good reason why I shouldn't kill you," shouted Oro. "Simple," choked Aan. "I am not your enemy; Vince is." Oro just stood there. He had no idea what to do, or who to believe.

Chapter Twelve-
Stop!

"Stop!" At first, no one heard the girl's voice. "STOP! What do you all think you're doing? STOP!" Oro slowly let Aan down. Aaron looked up. Ja turned his head slightly, keeping Stan in view. Seth smiled slowly. Nom was deep in thought. Ryan began yelling too. "Stop! Listen to her!" Dave and Max forgot they were fighting; they rushed out of the hall and into the Circle. Slay helped Mac up. Jordan and Vicky stopped their slashing, giving the other girls a chance to see Shelly. Jade Hira glanced around nervously, hoping to see that everyone had heard her.

"Look at you all," she began again. "Urumqi don't fight Urumqi. Agents don't fight Agents. How are you all going to stop the Empire? You can't all be planning on doing that once you're dead, can you? You know I used to think you were all so great for standing up against the Empire. But if all you can do is fight each other; well you're no better than them, are you? You know I lost my parents because of the Empire..." "She's right!" shouted Ja. Everyone grew silent. "You know I've always kept quiet, but I've had enough. I kept quiet when Oro tried to warn me about the Urumqi splitting up. I kept quiet when Aan kicked Jim out. I kept quiet when Ryan said that our purpose was to stop Oro instead of stopping the Empire."

Oro listened, mesmerized. He had never had the chance to know what Ja really thought. "You know I bet none of you knew..." continued Ja. "None of you knew that the Empire killed my parents too..." Oro was shocked. It was as if a shield that had been held up his whole life was suddenly dropped; it all made perfect sense. "When I joined the

Urumqi, I only hoped that I might give the Empire a few wounds in exchange. Instead, I found myself caught up in a squabble between two best friends. Aan, what were you thinking, man? Oro is your best friend and you forced him away from you. I think that the reason he left was because he knew that things ought to be set right. He knew how the Empire could rip away people's lives, right Jade? He tried to tell you, Aan, that there are people out there like me and Jade, who struggle through every day alone, just hoping to avenge their parents' death before they too become victims. I bet none of you know what that's like."

To be hurt
To feel lost
To be left out in the dark
To be kicked when you're down
To feel like you've been pushed around
To be on the edge of breaking down
With no one there to save you
If you don't know what that's like
Welcome to my life

"The point is that you all have to stop fighting. Learn to open your eyes," pleaded Jade to those who still wore malicious looks on their faces. "I know Oro has." She smiled at him. "When I first met him, he was fighting that Mando to protect me," she said, pointing at Aaron. "Now he's learned to move past that and fight alongside him. Why can't all of you learn to do that?" Oro looked at Aan. "How 'bout it?" "Sure thing," said Aan quietly, slapping Oro on the back. Everyone followed their lead, starting with Slay and Mac, who already felt stupid for fighting each other. Dave and Max were next, clasping their armored hands together. Aaron had tears in his eyes as he helped Zach up. With a wave of his staff, Ja helped Stan to his feet. Nom smiled as Wanda refused to take his hand, much too proud to receive any help getting up.

Without the knowledge of any of the people below, three men stood silently on the back rooftop, watching the Urumqi reunite. "Unbelievable," spat the first and youngest of the three. "I did everything perfectly. How can she undo the plans that I have made for the past year with only a few *words?*" The other two men hesitated. "Shall I..." prompted the second man, raising a longbow. "Yes, shoot her!" muttered the first man in a fit of rage.

Just then a fourth man scaled his way up onto the rooftops. Dan Carver lit his blaster, aligning its sight with the second man's body. The capsule struck him squarely in the chest; he breathed no more.

"No!" screamed Ja as the longbow's arrow struck Jade. With a speed faster than any in the lands of Uru, he jumped up onto the roof after the three men, his staff glowing blue. The third man, clad in solid metal plating, rushed him before he could see where the first man had gone. Ja sidestepped the attack and cracked his armor with a devastating blow to the back. Blood dripped down from the rooftop.

With a boost from one of his Mandos, Aaron pulled himself up onto the roof in time to throttle the warrior with the rest of the razor wire before he could get up. "Who is your friend who left? Who is he?" asked Aaron, pulling the wire tighter. "Guranqi," sputtered the warrior. "The Emperor's son..." The others all looked up at Ja, waiting to hear an explanation. "The one who ran was Derek," he said tersely. No one knew whether to be surprised or relieved. "From what Aaron forced this Imperial guard to tell him, Derek is Emperor Viron's son." "But what about Vince?" blurted Aan. "How did he know about the chest if he isn't a Guranqi?"

"Why don't you let me tell you," heaved Vince as he staggered out of the hallway, his shoulder bleeding painfully. "You dropped the note, Aan. The note from Ryan that said everything about the chest...you dropped it when you killed Nate Farelle. I misunderstood it to mean that the chest gave *you* power. I didn't understand that all you were trying to do was keep it away from the Empire. So naturally, I thought if we could take it..." "I get it," said Aan roughly. "Oh, one more thing," interjected Jim, who for the first time ceased to scowl at Seth. "I doubt many of you noticed, but Dan Carver, the guy who claimed he wouldn't help the Urumqi tonight, is right up there on the roof. Had he been there a second sooner, he would have killed that archer before that arrow hit Jade..." "Get down here, Dan!" called out Oro. Reluctantly, Dan jumped down from the roof to join his friends.

After giving everyone a few minutes to talk, Ryan succeeded in getting the large group quiet. "I think we owe it to ourselves to make sure that Jade and Shelly receive a proper burial. It is really a shame that..." "How about tomorrow?" offered Nom. "After tonight, I really doubt that we are going to have 'school.'" For the first time since becoming an Urumqi, Ryan laughed. "Okay, how about first thing tomorrow at the Park." "Sure thing," nodded Oro, knowing that he was automatically in charge of every get-together at the Park.

Dave lit up a few torches from the fire before it went out. The ragtag group of Agents, Mandos, Traditionals, Contemporaries, and Urumqi left West Side Temple[8] no longer hating, but accepting and understanding each other's differences. Wendy lifted Shelly's body, willing it to hover next to her for their quick jaunt to the Park. Ja did the same for Jade, tears running down his cheeks. At Oro's place, the group gave their not so final farewells as they all headed for home.

Chapter Thirteen-
An Unexpected Party

Shortly after this day, my father's life returned to normal, at least for the time being, that is. He has yet to tell me the rest of his story as I sit here writing these words now. As for what happened immediately after his 'Major Confrontations', here's what I like to believe...

Seth arrived first to the Park, even though there wasn't an exact time. Oro saw him sitting next to the lifeless bodies of Jade and Shelly as he stepped out of bed and looked through the window. Aan came next. Oro was surprised to see him carrying his usual box of 'party things' as well as his old four stringed guitar, which normally never left the Huila house. Ryan, Wanda, Slay, and Zach were right behind him, not quite so sure that a party would make things better. Of course Seth changed their minds when he popped open one of Aan's drinks and splashed it all over them.

By the time Oro got dressed and made it out of the house, Nom, Mac, and Max came running up from the East side, clearly hoping for a party as opposed to a funeral. Dave came next, bringing enough drinks to last him as he reverted back to his usual silly self. Jordan and Vicky came next, bringing a mismatched collection of rings, skins, and branches, which upon closer inspection by Oro, was revealed to be several hand made drums. Jim and Stan were close behind them; Jim also carried with him a battered looking guitar, while Stan carried what seemed to be a set of very, very old symbols. Trailing Stan was the Main Man and a few of his buddies.

Ava and Mandi came next, looking incomplete without Jade by their side. Wendy came too, hugging Aan as she saw Shelly. Vince walked up quietly, not wanting to draw attention to himself. Dan arrived looking better than he ever had, renewed confidence reflecting off of his once panic stricken smile. Ja was of course the last one to appear; yet he received the most attention because of his 'new way of thinking'.

"What do you think?" asked Ryan. "What would Shelly want us to do..." "No," said Ja simply. "Today is about Jade." The group stood silent. "I think I've got something," said Oro nervously, when it was clear that none of them had any ideas. "We've got enough music stuff...why don't we play her a little something." The group nodded their approval. Jim started off, playing nothing in particular, only what he felt like playing. Aan joined in, adding his part to the music, as did Vicky, Jordan, and whoever else was close enough to start in on the drums.

Thanks for all you've done
I've missed you for so long
I can't believe you're gone
You still live in me
I feel you in the wind
You guide me constantly
I never knew what it was to be alone, no
You were always there for me
You were always there waiting
Now I come home and I miss your face now
Smiling down on me; I close my eyes to see...
And I know...you're a part of me
I miss your song...for it set me free
I sing it while...I feel I can't go on
I sing tonight...for it comforts me

"That was great, Oro!" called out Vicky. Ja cut away a special place beneath the oak tree with his staff. Ava lifted

Jade into the freshly dug grave. Throwing in handfuls of dirt, they covered Jade's body. Off to the side, Aan dug a place for Shelly. As the mood wore off, Jim called out for another go. "How about something louder this time?" "Why not?" said Oro. "Are you sure you don't want to sing this time?" "Nah, Nah," said Jim quickly.

Walked away; heard them say:
Poisoned hearts will never change
Walked away again.
Turned away in disgrace,
Felt that chill upon my face
Cooling from within...
Hard to notice...gleaming from the sky
When you're staring at the cracks.
Hard to notice...what is passing by
With eyes lowered

Seth carefully planned his attack. He made the ice cold bucket of water hover above Oro's head for a few seconds before overturning it, drenching his friend unexpectedly. Bringing back life to the party, he tossed everyone a fresh round of drinks. There were no longer two groups, but one.

The next arrival took everyone by surprise. "I don't know if I have a right to be here," said Aaron coolly. "I don't know if Jade really forgave me for what I did. Heck, I don't even know if the Marahs will ever forgive me..." "It doesn't matter," said Oro kindly, "because we forgive you." The wind blew; Jade Hira's last wish came true.

Part Three-
The Mountains

Chapter One-
The Legend Continues

Oro sat on the cozy little sofa next to the crackling fire. As usual, Yia rested in her big oaken armchair, which was perfectly placed to be in reach of both the fire poker and the curio cabinet with the broken lock. "Don't fret over it, Oro. There's nothing you could have done..." "I could have saved her!" was Oro's vehement reply. "Ha. Let me tell you a little story. Remember how Tib Kanoka fled after betraying Ben to the first Emperor?" Oro nodded. "Well, at first he just ran; he ran as far away from Imperial City as he could; he kept running, but he couldn't outrun the memories of his brother that were chasing after him like ravenous wolves. Yeah, Tib felt pretty bad about what he did. For the rest of his not so lengthy life, he did everything he could to make it up to the Urumqi." "Does that mean I should try to avenge Jade's death?" "No, no. Tib was deathly afraid of Him. In fact, that's part of the reason he ran; if he had stayed, he would have surely been killed. No, Tib decided to give the Urumqi a different gift. He built the first Temple."

"And it wasn't just a Temple," continued Yia. "The place was alive with the power of the Qi." "But he was only one man...how could he build a Temple alone?" "Two reasons: first off, he wasn't alone. On his journey, he met a nice girl and eventually settled down and built that Temple. Second, he used his Urumqi power in the physical construction. It is one of two buildings ever to be constructed by sheer willpower." "Is this Temple still around today?" Yia laughed. "Of course it is...it's right at the Crossroads where it's always been." It all made sense now. Oro's Temple was the work of none other than the legendary Tib Kanoka. "So does that mean Tib made the secret hallway too? And the chest...?" "Quite right, you see...the chest was his greatest gift that he could give. It was a gift of hope. Inside, he placed the most beautiful sapphire that Uru ever forged. Tib knew that whoever opened the chest would feel the power that rested within." Oro remembered Vince's driving motivation to steal that very chest, not three weeks ago. "So what would have happened if we had opened the chest?" Yia shifted uneasily in her chair. "Nothing; nothing would have happened."

"I don't understand..." "I guess I better start from the beginning," laughed Yia, smiling widely. "When I was little, nearly all of the Urumqi were in hiding, and those who weren't were faced with constant harassment and bullying at the hands of Vora. My parents told me that I had the power to once again unite the Urumqi and to overthrow the Emperor. Being the foolish girl that I was, I believed every word my father told me. He said that I was the first girl in the Kanoka family to be an Urumqi; he told me to pass down the Kanoka name to my children. Well, I did just that. At the peak of things, I'd say I knew every single Urumqi, or at least the family names of the Urumqi, whose roots could be traced back to the folk of Olde. For awhile, we went unnoticed, sweeping across both the East and the West side, hoping to encircle Imperial City and squash it like a bug.

"But that hope faded when Viron came of age. His hatred and vehemence was like Vora's only tenfold. We knew he had the power to hurl every last rock and boulder in Uru at us before he would see the Urumqi overthrow the Empire. And so it was that he created the Elite, a team of Imperial soldiers that acted as his personal bodyguards. Eventually, we were forced to once again give up the entire East side. But we held them at the crossroads for a very long time; so long, in fact, that they grew tired of regrouping their army and pulled back to the City. I'm convinced that Tib's magic is what helped us hold the crossroads…"

"Anyway, Viron didn't stay puzzled for long. He soon realized that the Temple had something to do with our victory. He and his Elite attacked the Temple late one night; of course Viron found your secret passage…" "But why? I thought only Urumqi could see…" "He knew, he *knows*, how to think like an Urumqi. That is why he is so dangerous. That very night, I was in that secret room, holding council with a few of the other leaders. When they came, we knew right away something was different. His men no longer wore armor, only tattered brown cowls. They had no longbows, or scimitars, or knives. The only weapons they carried were long, double bladed swords. We all knew that Viron was trying something new. We held them back for as long as we could, but they overpowered us and took the chest." "What…" "One of us got cut off from the group. They took him and beat him brutally…he never returned…"

Silence. "Then they finally left; we had to figure out what to do. Knowing that the chest was an icon of hope, I suggested building a replica. The Urumqi who were not there that night never found out what happened…" "Do they know now? Who were your friends? Would I know any of them?" "No, they don't know…look, Oro, I can't tell you everything…you aren't ready yet." "But I have to do something now! Everyone is looking to me for leadership. There's got to be something you can tell me…" "Finish what I started, Oro. Make a plan; take apart the Empire one man at a time. Before you know it, there won't *be* an Empire." Oro smiled. There was no turning back now.

Chapter Two- Time to Regroup

Derek Drake waved his hand at the metal door so viciously that instead of sliding up, it tore completely off of its rusty track. "Father I failed. I failed! That Hira girl ruined everything! All she did was shout at everybody and rattle off a meaningless speech; and they all stopped fighting!" Viron flicked his sunken eyes up toward his son. "You did not expect to beat Kanoka the first time, did you?" Derek grew silent. It was obvious that he had not truly considered Oro's background. "I don't know. But I do know that the fighting is far from being over." "You mean the in-fighting, don't you?" "Yes, father. The ones who called themselves the outcasts will always distrust the by-the-book leaders like Ridder. Same goes for the Agents and the Mandos; regardless of how friendly Aaron Brown is with Oro's Agents, the animosity between the two groups as a whole is still powerful." "You seem to know these people better than I," mused Viron with praise. "Yes, father; I know them well." "So what is it you plan on doing?" "I believe that I should create a council of the Imperial leaders, father, and work with them to see how we can collectively overthrow our enemies." "Well planned, son. Just tell me who you wish to speak with and it will be done."

Oro and Nom walked slowly down the ancient trail behind the Patal house. "I think it's been long enough, don't you?" asked Oro. Nom hesitated before answering. "I just don't want to rush it, because that could refuel the fighting." "Yeah, but if we wait too much longer, there might be some consequences that we aren't prepared for. It could be like the Valley all over again." It was obvious that the time Nom had spent in the Valley was not as pleasant as Oro's. "Okay.

Tomorrow, Mac and I will come to your place and we'll round everyone up." "Sounds like a party," laughed Oro. "No," said Nom seriously, before cracking a smile.

The morning came sooner than it should have. Oro awoke to the blue-black horizon, just as the sun was about to open its weary eyes. The knocking at the door caused Oro to quickly throw on his clothes. "Nom, it's just way too early," he whined. "Nonsense!" called out Mac with too much alacrity. After rounding up Aan, Seth, and Ja (who happened to be staying over at Seth's place), they agreed to split up to make things go faster. Soon, they were all seated quietly around the old oak tree at the Park: Oro, Nom, Mac, Aan, Ja, Seth, Ryan, Zach, Slay, Ava, Mandi, Wendy, Wanda, Vince, Stan, Jordan, Vicky, and Jim; eighteen all together. "Anybody want to lead?" joked Ryan, rubbing his eyes groggily. "There aren't going to be any leaders, Ryan. The Urumqi should be a democracy," boomed Ja before anyone could answer. Oro wasn't yet used to Ja's new demeanor of speaking out. "Agreed," Ryan scoffed quickly. "So what's the first thing that we *collectively* plan on doing?" asked Jim, with a touch of sarcasm in his voice. "Well, the way I see it, we need to be absolutely sure that our allies, no matter what side they were on during the feud at the Temple, know that we are now one body. We need to know who can still be trusted," announced Oro.

This seemed to be the general consensus. "Let's start with the Agents," suggested Nom. "From what I can tell, Max and Dave are completely over their differences. I'm not as street smart as Stan, here, but am I correct to say that their clans account for nearly all of the Agents in Uru?" Stan slid uneasily off of his bench. "Well, you're always going to have a few independent guys out there, but for the most part, the Agents Clan is likely to be united by them and them alone." He cracked his knuckles. "While we're talking about our allies, I don't think there are any mysteries involving the Main Man and his…" "Who?" broke in Aan.

"The Traditionals' leader…" "You mean they actually have a leader?" laughed Ryan.

"Funny you should say that, Ryan," mumbled Vince. "I believe you once tried to find that 'leader' and it was obvious that you would fail." Ryan shot him a questioning look. "The Traditionals don't have 'leaders'," clarified Stan. "They're organized into groups based on who deals them their information. Nate Farelle was far from being a friend, but I believe that everything he told me was true. And assuming Farelle was right, the Main Man is the closest thing to a leader that we're gonna get; and an honest leader, at that." Nobody questioned Stan's insight.

"The Mandos are fairly easy…" broke off Oro as Vicky nudged him. He ignored her and went on. "Aaron Brown is no double-crosser. He and his men will remain allied with us as long as we continue to hire them…" "I heard something interesting concerning Aaron that I think you all should know about," interrupted Jim. "Dad let it slip that somebody real high up in the Imperial ranks wants Aaron dead. This person seems to be close enough to the Emperor to make it happen, should Aaron return to Imperial City." Oro was caught in the middle. He knew that almost everyone would not approve of giving Aaron a tip off to stay away from the City. He and Nom were the only ones who trusted him. But Oro knew that their help could mean the difference between victory and defeat, as was the case during the Battle of the Temple[1]. "Look, I know you all don't trust him, but if the Empire is planning on killing him, that should be enough proof for all of us that Aaron is on our side." As conversation broke out, Aan called out, "We'll discuss it later!" He nodded for Oro to continue. Oro was glad that his feud with Aan was over.

"The final faction that we must discuss is the Contemporaries…Ryan can handle that, I think," prompted Oro. "To put it quite simply," began Ryan, "the Big Man isn't so big anymore. He's lost nearly all of his guards, all of his clients, and, if he doesn't start turning things around, all of his money. I think that it would be the right thing to do to help him out enough just to keep his businesses going. That way, if he ever becomes 'Big' again, we can cash in a few favors. As for the rest of the Contemporary community, I doubt they respect him anymore. Once they see that we rebels actually have a fighting chance, they'll jump right in and fight alongside us to take back their tax money from the Empire."

Satisfied with Ryan's explanation, Nom finished things up by figuring out when to meet the next day and who ought to come. "Stan, see if you can get the Main Man to come by, and see if he knows where Aaron is. Ryan, have the Big Man come. I'll make sure Max and Dave are going to show up. Am I missing anyone?" "Yeah, Dan," said Jim quickly. "Of course," beamed Nom. "Oh yeah, not so early next time," laughed Stan. "How 'bout around noon?"

Chapter Three-
The Councils

Derek eyed each man that was seated around the conference chamber somewhere in the bowels of the ancient City. The first, and certainly the oldest, was the Guran himself. As a young boy, when Derek first saw the Guran, he was instantly afraid. The deep scar along his face, the missing fingers, and the gnarled calf infused with a metallic crutch-foot made him appear to be a revered warrior. In reality, he was. The Guran was the pure embodiment of all that the Guranqi stood for. His job was to train the young adepts until they too were powerful warlords. This position alone gave him a right to be on the council.

Taking up at least two chairs, the second man was nothing short of behemoth, towering above the others even when seated. He was the commander and chief of the Grand Imperial Army. To his right was a metal-clad warrior about half the size. He was the commander of the Elite, the Special Task Force of the Empire. His men specialized in one-on-one combat and more versatile fighting styles, making them useful for taking out key leaders during battles. Across from him was a greasy, wiry little man with huge sunken eyes and jet black hair. He was the Imperial Tech. He played the role of both scientist and inventor. The final member of Derek's council was a hardened looking man, laden with weapons of all sorts, some of which the other commanders had never seen before. He was Viron's personal assassin and lead Mando; for Aaron no longer served the Empire through the Guran as he had done in the past.

"I have discovered first hand that it will take more than fell words and trickery to stop Kanoka," boomed Derek, getting everyone's attention. "Although the Urumqi may not be a direct threat, the fact that we cannot easily destroy them is what makes them dangerous." The others just stared at him with blank expressions. Only the Guran knew where this was going. "Think about it, Gorath," said Derek, nodding toward the commander and chief. "If there was an army out there that was considered untouchable, wouldn't it drive you mad to allow them to go unchallenged when you know *you* are the best?" "Aye, sir. Wish to eradicate every last one of them, I would," he rumbled. "You too, Igni," continued Derek. "If there was a Task Force out there who claimed they were better than you, would you just let them have all the glory?" "Never!" The word shot from his mouth like an icy wind, threatening to freeze anything that opposed it. Gorath shifted uneasily in his seat. "Very well, I think you now understand my predicament. If I cannot find a way to control the Urumqi, I am no better than a worthless rabble trying to control my pigs!" The listeners responded with their consent. "Together, how should we defeat the Urumqi?"

None save the Guran were expecting such an open ended question. "I think I have an idea," rasped the Guran once it was obvious that no one else would respond. Derek nodded for him to continue. "I have always been fascinated with the history of our beginnings. I really think it's too bad that my predecessors didn't take better care in leaving behind their legacies; specifically the Gurans that knew Him." Derek smiled, for he knew what the old man wanted. "If we take a legion to the mountains and find His grave, I believe that we will come across much more than a long dead body." "What makes you think there's something of value in the mountains?" asked the man with the weapons. "Well, Qur'shan, if you were a Guranqi, I could show you." Turning to Derek, the old man said, "Lower your shields.

Search the land. Feel the presence of the Qi. Only if you do that can you truly understand what I mean."

Derek hated opening his mind, but he did so anyway. Slowly, the dark conference room faded away. His mind now read from feelings, instead of vision. Next to him, the Guran appeared yellow, for he was closely linked with the Qi. Igni and Qur'shan shone orange. Derek struggled to see beyond the room. His mind became a map of Uru, stretching further and further out. "Ah," he coughed, as a pain surged through his head. The Guran smiled. "When I look there, I no longer feel the pain, but I cannot see what lies beyond. It is as if someone or something with a stronger will than I is guarding the mountains from foresight." Intrigued by the idea of a powerful artifact, Derek asked, "Does the chest that we stole give off any power?" The Guran's face fell. "No."

The eighteen Urumqi, two Agents, a Mando, a Traditional, a Tech, and a Contemporary sat together in the solitude of the Park. The Agents were, of course, Max and Dave, as was the Mando Aaron. The Traditional was the Main Man himself, as was Dan the Tech. The Contemporary was more of a mystery; only Aan recognized him, for he had seen him during his first visit with the Big Man. His name was Banda.

"Look, I know we've been friends for a long time," said Dave uneasily. "...but your path is far different from ours. We must continue to pursue our careers in the event that the Empire *doesn't* fall at your hands. If some evil should befall you, it would be a shame for all of our Agents to fall down with you." No one could deny the logic of his statement. "I don't understand," said Oro, faking confusion. "During our little skirmish, both of you gladly took up sides without even thinking of the casualties or the consequences. Now, *now* when its time to unite against a common enemy, you refuse? If the people of Uru cannot unite under a single banner to bring an end to this tyranny, who can? You can hardly look to us if, like you said, something evil should befall us." Max glanced at his comrade. "Okay, but next time you pay us. If you need us, we claim our share of the reward." "Agreed!" beamed Nom.

"It's hardly fair that the same terms apply to me," scraped Aaron's chilling voice. "My men are now seventeen; three were lost in your little skirmish. And…I am almost certain we have been discovered by the Empire. We dare not return to the City, and out here, we have no way of making money." Glad that Aaron already knew the danger of Imperial City, Oro offered a suggestion. "I'm sure you know the entire City better than anyone else in Uru. Why don't you act as our inside man and discover new ways to assault the Empire?" Aaron's crooked smile returned to his face. "I guess I could do that. Might as well hit 'em where it hurts." Silence. "We'd appreciate that, man," called out Nom sincerely. "If you ever need any help, you know to look to us as allies." Aaron respectfully pointed a gloved finger at Nom, in the customary way for Mandos. With that, he departed.

"So, Banda," sneered Aan when it was obvious no one else planned on continuing. "I'm sorry to hear that your Master is going through a rough patch." "Don't talk to me like I'm an ignorant fool," snapped the dark skinned guard. "I know that it was your fault that he lost so much," he boomed, jabbing an accusing finger at Ryan. "Hold it, calm down, he didn't mean to offend," hollered Wanda. "You're here because we *want* to help you." Banda stood silent. "If we can find a way to finance ourselves, we will gladly give your Master a loan in the interest of him supporting us when it truly becomes time to assault the Empire," offered Seth. Banda laughed. "That's no deal! I know how much product you stole from us at the Coast. If anything, you *owe* us money." "Has anyone else offered to help you, huh?" shouted Jim, obviously frustrated by being accused. "Yeah, I didn't think so. Take it or leave it, buddy." Banda had heard enough; he promptly left.

Jim took a deep breath. "You have anything to add, Dan?" All eyes turned to the Tech, yet he continued to remain quiet. 'I should have come sooner. I could have killed that archer. I thought it was the right thing to do to put my family above my friends…but now I've let everyone down…' Snapping back to reality, he considered Jim's question. "What more can I say? There's already one blaster out there that's out of my control, and to make things worse, my parents want to market them! They don't get it…nobody gets it." None of them had ever seen him so sad. It suddenly made sense why Dan was here. He was not a Traditional, and certainly not a Contemporary. He hated the Empire, yet his parents supported it. That left him only one choice: be with the Urumqi or be alone.

Chapter Four-
The Army

Just as the Urumqi were about to depart from the Park, a great commotion up on the road followed by several yells caused the group to retreat farther into the trees. "I'm going to go see what that is," mouthed Ja to the group. Ghostlike, he leapt through the shadows and between the trees until he reached the ditch alongside the West Road. "Come on! Can't you guys let me through here? It will only take a minute," pleaded a man. "Let us pass first," said another voice, this one more official. "But my cart is too heavy to move off of the road…" The first man tumbled off the road and into the ditch, landing dangerously close to Ja. A line of blood dribbled across his face. Even more curious now, Ja climbed just high enough to get a distorted view of the road. What he saw was a site like none other. Lining the road eight abreast were nearly six hundred soldiers, several of which were shoving their victim's cart off of the road. After they finished, their captain called for them to continue marching.

Ja sprinted back to the group and reported what he had just seen. Chaos instantly broke out. After several minutes, it came down to whether the issuing of the army should alter their current plans. "We need to know what they're up to," insisted Vicky. "Don't you have any idea how many lives could be lost, how many families could be broken if they choose to attack…if they go unchecked?" Nobody could argue with her. Becoming an Urumqi creates a special connection between parent and child; no longer would family be taken for granted. It was for this very reason that Oro felt he had been cheated. The ultimate conclusion was to have Ja follow the army to their camp for the night, giving the rest of the Urumqi time to return home for necessary supplies. It had taken awhile for Oro to get used to the idea that Ja had no family. Even so, Oro couldn't help but wonder what his home was like.

Emperor Viron sat alone in his throne room. He stretched out with his mind as he struggled to see his vast kingdom all at once. To the North his mind fell upon the wasteland that was the Empire's wake. Each year, his kingdom moved a bit closer to the South as the fell poison of his industries made the land uninhabitable. To the South, his mind fell upon Tib's Temple, the invincible stronghold. He followed the West Road, beginning at the Temple, winding its way up into the hills. And then his conscious flashed white; bewildered, he returned to his throne room. His son was right. Some sort of anomaly existed in those mountains. And, more importantly, the Guran knew of this and kept quiet. 'Old Vora was right; Guranqi can't be trusted,' he thought.

Oro tore open the front door, raced upstairs to find some parchment, and proceeded to write a note to his parents. *Mom and Dad- There is some pressing Urumqi business that I must personally oversee. I will be gone for as long as necessary. Take care of things for me. Love Oro.* Tossing the note onto the kitchen counter, he hurried back out the door, for he wanted to have as much time as possible to visit Yia before he had to meet up with the others. Reaching her house in record time, Oro explained to his grandma what Ja had seen. "Why would they send troops into the mountains? Not even the Emperor's men can survive up there," commented Oro. Yia took her time to answer. "The mountains are not really dangerous. In my opinion, people blow things out of proportion. One person sees a big snake and before you know it, it turns into a dragon by the tenth time the story is told." Oro laughed. He knew this was true. "However, there is something I must warn you about. I suspect that there is a specific reason why Vora avoided the mountains during his entire reign; a reason more terrifying than 'dragons'. My personal thought is that the Qi is strong there. All the nature that He forced out of Uru now dwells in those mountains. Do nothing to upset that nature, Oro." After gathering a few things that he would need for the journey, he hugged Yia goodbye and set out for the Park, where he was to meet the others.

The band of Urumqi set out down the road toward the towering mountains. No one talked. By nightfall, the group could see Ja's fire. Oro hoped that the flames could not be seen by the brigade of soldiers. They trudged on until they reached the little camp that Ja had set up. After receiving a quick update from him that the army was camped at a fork in the road just ahead, they began to unpack their blankets and get ready for sleep. Seth offered to take watch for the first half of the night. Drink in his hand, he prepared himself for six hours of solitude. The sun fell quickly behind the mountains; darkness fell earlier than usual. Wendy curled up next to Aan, squeezing his shoulder affectionately. Stan sat with his arms drawn up around his knees, leaning partially against a tree. Trying to ignore the confused looks from Jordan, he stared up at the horizon where the sun was quickly sinking. For the first time in front of the others, Oro and Vicky shared a kiss. Somehow it was different. Ever since that day at the coast, Vicky had been acting almost distant toward him. "I bet you two are going to sleep tight," joked Nom. "I got second shift; no different than home, eh!"

Oro dreamt that night. He stood before a wall, indefinitely long, high and thick. No matter how hard he tried, he couldn't break through to the other side. Then suddenly, a bright light shone and a being came through to Oro's side of the wall. The being was both good and bad, both beautiful and disgusting. No matter how hard he tried, he could not force it back through the wall. He awoke. Glancing around, everyone was still. Oro pulled Vicky closer and tried hard to fall back asleep.

For three more days they traveled, following the army higher into the hills. The temperature grew increasingly colder; food became hard to find. So hard, in fact, that Jim decided to create a contest as to who could provide the most food for the group. Ja was unnaturally skilled at hunting live animals. Over the three day period, he had killed two deer and some sort of goat-like animal. Second best was Nom, who had thrown a small rock and brought down some kind of bird, which surprisingly had enough meat for an entire meal. Oro found it interesting to watch how each Urumqi went about their daily routine. Unlike the Imperial soldiers, no two people did the same thing in the same order with the same method. An easy solution to one Urumqi was an impossible feat to another. 'This is what the Empire doesn't have,' thought Oro.

On the fourth morning, everything changed. "Where's Stan?" yelled Jordan, waking the entire group. "Shut up," seethed Ryan. "Do you want to alert the entire army that they're being followed?" "But where would he have gone?" she persisted. Although nearly everyone was as worried as she, they held their fear inside. Nobody had a good answer. Once the sun was high in the sky, they came dangerously close to the legion of troops. "What have they stopped for?" mused Ryan, as he motioned for everyone to retreat a ways so as not to be seen. "I'll go find out," whispered Ja. He was off before Ryan could tell him to stop. Sneaking to the outskirts of the rocky platform, he recognized the soldier who had killed the man with the wagon on the West Road. "When I say stop, we STOP!" he bellowed at another soldier, who stood his ground. "This is the place where he ordered us to go." The other man cut in, "How can you be sure?" "He told me exactly what to look for: a cave surrounded by stone walls on a rest in the road. Does this place not fit that description?" The other man silently slinked away. "Onward," bellowed the soldier, and the entire group slowly filed into a cave that opened from the clearing.

Ja reported back to the Urumqi. "Perfect. Let's force a few boulders into that cave and they'll be stuck forever," suggested Jim before anyone else could respond. "But who says we want to trap them? It's obvious they're going after something of value," replied Ava. It had been a long time since Oro had heard her voice. "I could scout out the cave and see if I can find whatever it is they're after," offered Ja. "No!" commanded Nom suddenly. "There is something...not right about this place." He glanced around to see if anyone agreed. The nodding of heads told him to continue. "I think I know why Stan left. Those dreams we've been having? You all had them, right?" More nodding. "There's something, I mean, someone in these mountains who is very powerful. Stan was *scared* away." Nobody could deny the truth of this. "So..." prompted Vince. "I'd bet that if we spent the night camped out up there on that rest, the dream might be more clear," suggested Nom. "Well, I guess we have no other choice," finalized Oro. And so they waited for nightfall.

Chapter Five-
Caliphia

It seemed to Oro that he fell asleep faster than usual. Before him was no longer a wall, but a...nothing. There was no way to describe where she came from; she appeared out of the nothingness. "Oro," she whispered softly. "Who are you?" he asked, frightened. "No need to be scared, Oro. I will not harm you. It is you whom I wish to speak with." Although she whispered in the softest tone, the way she said *I* sent a chill down Oro's spine. "What do you want?" he asked, this time more kindly. "I seek nothing more than your audience. When you wake, enter my cave and follow the light." With those words she vanished, and Oro awoke with a jolt. After checking that the others remained sleeping, he quickly dressed and stumbled his way over to the cave. Ryan was keeping watch, but somehow Oro swept past him unnoticed. Upon entering the cave, he saw a light. He followed it for what seemed like ages until he arrived in a candle lit chamber with two chairs. One was empty; she sat in the other one. She looked far less ethereal than she did in the dream, yet there was still a sense of divineness about her.

As he entered, she looked up at him and smiled. "It's about time you made it. Were you enjoying the scenery?" "I...um..." The sincerity of her voice caused Oro to snap out of his daze. "It's alright. I wasn't expecting an answer," she laughed softly. "There's a first time for everything. I'm Caliphia," she whispered, offering Oro her hand. Her touch was the softest thing Oro had ever felt. After an eternity, she met his gaze. "You know why you're here, I'm sure?" she asked. "No, not exactly," admitted Oro. "For starters, my home is being invaded by nearly six hundred soldiers led by a Guranqi, whom your company seems to be following."

Oro couldn't help but snicker at the bluntness of her statement. "Did you say a Guranqi?" asked Oro, snapping back to reality. "Yes; the Emperor's son to be more exact." Oro could tell that he was starting to go crazy. "How do you know all this about me and the army and the Guranqi? And how did you talk to me in a *dream*?"

"I guess I better explain from the beginning. My people and I have long lived in isolation from any facet of the outside world. We have chosen to rise above the things that plague the rest of the world and to be at peace with nature and with the Qi. Since the coming of your kind to Uru, we have been forced to choose between following our traditional ways, or living in a more direct harmony with those around us." "The Urumqi have always lived in Uru!" he interjected before she could finish. She met his eyes again. "How did the Guranqi come, Oro?" "On ships," he answered. "So is it not possible that having been here longer, we could say the same of you?" "I suppose," resigned Oro, "but then how did you get here?" She laughed softly, breaking the tension. "I guess I will never be lucky enough to know.

"Now as I was saying, I believe that if our peoples do not work together to defeat the Guranqi, there will be dire consequences." "Not to be irreverent," smiled Oro, "but why are you choosing to help us instead of the Guranqi? You say that we both came here on ships to make your life miserable…" "If *you* had marched in here with an army, I would have helped *them*…" She paused. "No, the reason I chose you is because you are the only one who accepted me. What you saw in your dream…it was nothing more than a test to see who would accept my people for who we are. Every one of them cringed when they saw that demon come through the wall. But to you, it was just as beautiful as it was ugly. Remember, Oro, be accepting of everyone, no matter who they are or what they believe…"

He now knew that he could trust her. "What can we do to assist you?" Oro asked. She gave him a resigned look. "I'm not yet sure that you fully understand our...my predicament. My people are on the brink of war, whether the Elders choose to acknowledge it or not. We must find a way to force them to realize that the Lehdeo are not the only beings who walk the valleys of Uru." Although her tone was calm, Oro could sense a tone of desperation in her voice. "Who are the Elders? What's the Lehdeo?" he asked. "We are the Lehdeo, Oro. The Assembly of Elders are those of us who have been endowed with the rights to make all of the decisions." "And does this Assembly include you?" "No...Oro, you must tell your followers what you have learned tonight. Tell them that they all must come before the Assembly and tell them that Uru will be destroyed if the Guranqi are not stopped." "And will it?" Caliphia looked deeply into Oro's eyes. "Only you can answer that question."

An icy wind howled through the tunnels, ruffling the tail of the blonde man's cloak. Derek Drake hated this place; it was like when he opened his mind, only this was a physical reality. Most of all, he hated the freezing wind; he knew he was far into the network of caves, yet the weather told him that this was impossible. He took another look around. The floors were slick with wet moss and algae. The walls were of a similar state, as was the ceiling, which was almost too high to see clearly. He knew that something wasn't right. At the speed he was running, he should have been half way across Uru by now; but somehow he was still in the mountains. A few hours ago, he had tried doubling back to meet up with his troops; he had no sooner rounded a single wide turn, and there they were. Somehow, he was going in circles; and he couldn't open his mind without terrible pain. Derek Drake had had enough.

In desperation, he plunged his hand into the inside wall. The wall was not made of rock. His eyes told him that it was, but his hand proved his eyes wrong. He forced himself through the wall, only to find another empty tunnel, this one less wet. He walked across the width of the tunnel and tried again. The third tunnel had no water or algae or slime. Farther and farther he worked his way inward until "rock" tunnels gave way to "wooden" hallways with soft flooring, and candles for light. Now he knew he was making progress, one way or another…

"Good…good!" rasped the Guran as he watched his favorite student knock her opponent to the ground. "I'm glad you think so," she said, "Because that wasn't a move that you taught me…Does this mean I'm done for the day?" "Not quite…" The Guran lifted his own sword, and with machine-like reflexes swung a lethal slash at his favorite student. She only just blocked the blow in time. Staggering backwards, she understood what her teacher meant. "That's the move you used on your opponent, was it not?" asked the old man. She nodded. "Yet you have no idea how to properly defend against such an attack," he spat condescendingly. "Never wield a power which you yourself cannot control," he commanded. Stepping forward, he pointed at his right shin, where the remainder of his calf muscle was infused with the shining gleam of the prosthetic crutch. Kira had learned her master's lesson.

When Oro was finally free of the twists and turns of Caliphia's cave, he found that it was nearly sunrise. Looking across the makeshift camp, it seemed that most were still sleeping. Nom sat atop a large boulder, eerily gazing towards home; he was too far away to notice Oro. Across the clearing, Jordan sat alone, dangling her feet off of the cliff and watching the first rays of sunshine. Oro joined her. For what seemed like forever, they stared out into the horizon. "Why did he LEAVE me?" she burst out suddenly, tears running down her cheeks. She was shaking uncontrollably. Oro put his arm around her and she calmed down a bit. "Whatever you do, you can't look at it like the whole thing is your fault…" he offered. "This place is scary.

Those *dreams* were scary. Maybe it just affected him a little more than you and me. You shouldn't blame yourself." Jordan knew he was right, but she couldn't bring herself to understand. Watching from her doubled-over sleeping mat, Vicky's face grew hot with anger.

Once all of the Urumqi were awake, Oro called for a quick meeting. "I have discovered what the dreams mean," began Oro. "And..." prompted Jim. Oro couldn't think of how to explain to them that they were camping on the doorstep of the Lehdeo. "In that cave," pointed Oro, "lives an entire civilization of Qi sensitive beings called the Lehdeo. Last night I was invited through a dream to meet with one of them. She says that we should speak before their ruling Assembly and tell them that we will need their help to destroy the Guranqi." "So we're trying to get an ally here?" asked Aan. "Have they already destroyed that army?" asked Ryan.

Oro felt a bit bombarded. "Yes, we are trying to gain an ally here; but I don't think that it will be easy. It seems that there are two factions within these Lehdeo people. Some of them want to live a life apart from the rest of Uru, while others wish to help the people of Uru. I believe that it is because of this difference that no hostile action against the army has been taken." "Great, more factions!" joked Mac. "So you're saying that six hundred soldiers, in addition to the Lehdeo people, are in that cave right now?" The group fell silent; Oro hesitated before speaking. "I think that the cave...I think that it moves."

"Huh?" was the general response. "I think that the cave is a work of the Qi. I think that they control its shape; no, I think they control its very existence," clarified Oro. "It's possible..." commented Nom, "perhaps a little Tib magic." Oro was surprised to find that most of them didn't know what Nom was referring to. "Well, are we gonna do this?" called out Aan. "After you, Oro," laughed Seth.

Chapter Six-
The Lehdeo

The man seemed to have appeared out of nowhere. He was rather skinny, with bony forearms that hung out of his extra large sleeves. He was dressed in a royal-looking cloak with gems embroidered right into the edges, giving him the appearance of a king who is down on his luck. "Ahh, the Urumqi," he said airily, greeting them with a formal bow. "We have been expecting you." He waited for a response, but received seventeen blank stares. "Do come along," he finished slowly, starting off down the hallway.

As the Urumqi followed the wiry man into the heart of the mountains, Oro tried to decide if he had been in this hallway before. The answer was yes and no; the mouth of the cave served as the entrance to only one tunnel, yet after only a few steps he found himself in an entirely different room than before, this one much larger, and decorated elegantly. Although not as massive as the Great Circle back home, this room was still too big for Oro to take in everything at once. The focal point of the chamber was a rectangular oaken table, complete with fifty high-backed wooden chairs, each one filled by a single man. Glancing upward, Oro noticed a multitude of tiered balconies, where the common folk could observe the Assembly meetings. On a high veranda above the head of the table, Caliphia stood, smiling down on him. Instantly, he was renewed with confidence.

The wiry man cleared his throat. "At this time, the Assembly of the Lehdeo recognizes the delegation of...Urumqi." A hush fell over the room. Every man seated at the table was silent; every person watching from above became quiet. The Urumqi stood in their loose formation, not daring anything other than silence. The bald man seated at the head of the table quietly stood up. "Which one of you will be speaking on behalf of your faction?" he called. Although his words formed a question, his demeanor expressed a demand. "We all shall speak. We are a democracy!" boomed Ja, startling a few of the council members. "Very well," said the leader. "To begin, am I correct in saying that you are here because of this...army that has trudged onto our lands?" "Yes; we wish to prevent them from causing any harm," answered Oro. "Now why would you believe that they would harm anyone within your own kingdom? Are you not a part of the kingdom that this army is told to protect?" "It is our destiny to destroy the Guranqi," explained Aan. "What do the Guranqi have to do with this army? There are no Guranqi here; only *you*," the leader said sharply.

"I believe you are mistaken, sir," noted Oro in the kindest tone possible. "There is a Guranqi here, for the army *is* that of the Guranqi." Silence. "That army is a battalion of our kingdom, our Empire if you will. The Guranqi have controlled this Empire ever since its dawn," clarified Oro. "So then is it correct for me to say that, considering your obvious ability to control the Qi and your association with this...Empire, you yourself are a Guranqi?" scoffed the leader. Aan was outranged by the question. "No! No, we are Urumqi..." he offered.

Oro couldn't help but be surprised by the general confusion of nearly every member of the assembly. They were all pointing and whispering to each other, as if clarifying what Aan had said. "Allow me to explain," grumbled a gray bearded man at the other end of the table. "Before you arrived here in the mountains, the *popular* belief was that the *true* Urumqi of Olde, as you would call them, became...extinct with the coming of the first Guran from the sea." Oro could tell that this man was different from the others. Although he spoke gruffly, there was something reassuring in his voice. "It is obvious now that this belief is completely false, for here you stand before the council just like your ancestors did in the past," continued the bearded man.

"Enough of my rambling...now that you are here, there is something that we must..." The wiry greeter burst into the council chamber. "Sir, there's been a disturbance in the Southeast corner," he spewed hysterically. "One of...one of THEM is down there..." he wavered, pointing an accusing finger at the Urumqi. "Well, I think that settles any disputes," boomed the gray bearded man. "The Guranqi that they speak of has indeed broken through our defenses..." "First things first," interrupted the bald man. "Everyone stay put! Send someone down to that corner." His cold eyes burned into Oro's. "But if we catch him now, we could prevent an entire war!" explained Nom. "This may be the only chance we have to catch him alone, without the interference of the other Guranqi."

From high above, Oro heard the thunderous applause of the onlookers. 'Now the people see the assembly's inability to make decisions,' he thought. Ja stepped closer to the bald man's chair. "Allow us to go, and we *will* catch the Guranqi. Forbid us, and you shall be captured as well." Jim and Vicky stepped up to join him, as did Seth and Mac. Ryan, Slay, and the others took a few steps back. Only Nom seemed to waver, shifting slowly toward the nearest corridor. Oro remembered what Caliphia had told him. The Lehdeo were peaceful people, but their power lies in the mind. But it was already too late. With a slight nod of the bald man's head, Ja's supporters fell unconscious to the ground.

Chapter Seven-
The Fall of the Counselor

Nom dashed away from the council table and into the nearest hallway. He didn't know which way was Southeast, but the taint in the Qi that now emanated from Derek Drake was strong enough for him to follow.

"How...how..." sputtered the bald man as Ja continued to move closer. "Do not fool yourself," said Ja darkly. "I *am* you."

Aan approached the gray bearded man cautiously. "Look, we really don't want any trouble," he whispered. "Help us get out of here." The bearded man laughed. "Not before you help us take care of our little problem," he answered, glancing at the bald man.

With a slight nod to Ryan and Wanda, Aan pulled out his staff. The remainder of the group faced the bald man. Most of the assembly members were already out of their chairs, glancing nervously between the Urumqi and their leader. The gray bearded man stood. "Step down," he uttered, "Leave the position of High Counselor behind you...you know this..." "Enough; silence him," wailed the bald man. A roar erupted from the onlookers as a bolt of white energy shot from Vince's staff, striking the bald man with unnatural accuracy. The bald man did not waver. "You are indeed foolish to take up arms against me!" he screamed. Sitting down, his metallic blue eyes seared through Vince's mind.

Oro watched as Vince writhed in agony on the floor. "Release him NOW." The words tore through the cavernous room like a title wave. The gray bearded man pointed a gnarled finger at Oro. "Help me," he said. Oro now understood what Caliphia had told him. Power does not lie in a physical blow; it lies in one's mind. Sitting cross legged on the floor, he concentrated on the situation at hand. His mind faded into a lightened sea of thoughts. He could see the bald man's resistance, a piercing red glow of stagnant smoke in a sea of white. He reached out with his own thoughts as he sought to clear the crimson glow.

Nom Patal could tell that he was deep below ground. He wasn't sure how, but he just knew. Cavernous hallways gave way to smaller corridors. 'This must be where the people live,' thought Nom. The tiny hallways were lit by candles hanging from brackets on the wall. The walls were made of wood, and seemed to be slightly damp. Feeling close to the darkness, Nom thought it best to wait. A great rumbling could be heard in the distance. As he waited, the sound grew nearer. Nom turned; he was face to face with Derek. The Guranqi had seemingly come out of nowhere. "You are foolish to confront me alone…in this place of ancient darkness," said Derek. With a wave of his pale hand, Nom found himself being crushed against the damp wall, his breath being slowly crushed out of him.

Nom struggled to pull his hand free from the flat surface. After several futile efforts, he succeeded in lifting a single finger from the damp wood. Derek flew backward, his omnipresent hold broken. Nom whipped out his oaken staff and gave it a sharp wave. Derek slid roughly across the floor. Nom could feel a strange power at work. Someone in these caves wanted him to succeed. Another wave of the oaken staff sent the Guranqi hurtling through the air. Upon his fall, Nom heard a sickening crack.

Deep within Imperial City, the Guran balanced himself on the three claws that served as his right foot. He cautiously opened his mind and looked to the mountains. It was evident that Derek was in trouble. The powerful force at the heart of the mountains was somehow working against him. 'Unbelievable!' he thought. 'Run, Derek, run!'

Nom delivered another blow, and then another. Derek writhed in pain on the musty floor, his left forearm badly broken. Using the last of his strength, the Guranqi pulled himself across the floor and grabbed hold of the virtual wall through which he had appeared. Ripping himself through the mysterious barrier, he breathed a sigh of relief when he discovered that Nom was unable to follow. He knew that he had to return to Imperial City; nothing else mattered.

The bald man knew that the end was near. With each passing minute, his power waned. 'Why is it…that they don't understand? The Urumqi…and Guranqi…they are the same…' The last breath rolled from his lungs. The four unconscious Urumqi slowly stood. Nom slipped in silently from the hallway. A cheer erupted from the terraces and balconies above. "You have helped me accomplish a great feat today," began the bearded man, looking right at Oro. "You have helped my people to remember the ancient glory of the Urumqi. I believe that you have given us a reason to join the outside world, not hide from it!" he beamed. "So you will help us to defeat the Guranqi?" clarified Oro, before the older man could go any further.

The Urumqi knew the answer long before the words were spoken. "You must understand…" whispered the bearded man sadly. "Our choice to invite you here, to ally with you against the will of the High Counselor…it has never been done in the history of the Lehdeo. What we have done today…is already an unthinkable step forward. It would be foolish for you to ask us to leave our home for the sake of your war." None of them knew what to say, for the old man's argument was more than valid. "What of the army?" asked Ryan. "Let's just say I don't think you'll be seeing them anytime soon," laughed the bearded man. "Thank you, and we go in peace," said Aan with a hint of formality.

As the party headed for the mouth of the cave, the vague line between victory and defeat had already faded into a fog of uncertainty. "They aren't going to help us," said Ryan, while the group packed their things. "AND we never found out about the cave, AND we have no idea why Derek led his army up here, AND I let him get away," breathed Nom dangerously. "It isn't your fault that he escaped, man; he escaped all of us that night at the Temple…" offered Oro. "I'm not saying it's my fault, I'm saying it's everyone else's fault for not helping me get him," replied Nom caustically. Oro had never seen Nom get so upset. "Let him whine about it," spat Vicky. "There's nothing you could have done, oh wait, you could have helped me when I was struck unconscious on the floor!"

"That's not fair to blame him like that!" snapped Jordan. "Don't you get it that he's the reason we're all alive?" She stopped. "We're just going to leave him here?" Tears rolled down her cheeks as she thought about Stan. Oro gave her a quick squeeze. "Remember all those little tricks he taught me to keep my staff away from the guards?" She smiled. "Yeah." "Well I don't think that anything or anyone in the mountains will stand a chance against him. He'll make it out okay."

As much as Oro wanted to believe that Stan would come back, he knew that his encouraging words were only a quick fix. As he looked back on the last few days, he wondered what he was missing at home. 'What have I done? I left them all…' He had a nasty feeling that the trip to the mountains was not the right move…

Chapter Eight-
The Plot

Viron sat peacefully in his throne room. It had taken only minimal effort to fix the door that his son had violently broken. 'His power was truly great.' Breaking his train of thought, the Guran strode into the room. "What is it?" snapped Viron irritably. "I have reason to believe that the Urumqi are not here," rasped the old man slowly. "What do you mean? Speak," insisted Viron. "They have followed Derek into the mountains. As you know, your son has been gone for nearly five days now. I believe that it will be at least four more days until his return, if not longer. It would give us time to militarize nearly all of the East side and much of the West side before their return."

He paused. "Personally, I was rather surprised by the lack of conflict over your decree to force the younglings into schools. And that happened with the current Urumqi right here in Uru. Imagine the progress I could make if you order martial law to contain an 'Urumqi outbreak'..." hissed the Guran, clicking his steel crutch against the stone floor. "I agree with you, Guran, although it's too bad that Derek won't get to kill them himself," mused Viron. "Not to say that he isn't up for the challenge," crackled the Guran ironically, "but why put him at risk when you have a whole army of soldiers willing to die for you?" "Fair enough, old man," rumbled Viron. "Tell Gorath to *first* march his men to the foot of the mountain. There must be no way for the Urumqi to escape." The Guran turned. "I was planning on appointing Igni to guard the West Road. Gorath will have his hands full..." Scraping his way towards the door, the old man wondered if Derek would make it home alive.

"I will be home for dinner," chuckled Nom's grandma as she opened the oaken front door and headed out to the trail. A short ways down the dusty path, she found Yia, who was arbitrarily watering a worn out looking rose bush, using the Qi to carry water to it from a muddy looking puddle. The two women smiled. "What're you doing?" she asked beaming. "That plant's as good as dead, Yia." "Every year you tell me that…" began Yia. "And every year it survives, I know," replied Mrs. Patal. "Enough small talk; what news do you have for me?" Suddenly, Yia's demeanor changed. "I think that the time has come. Our grandsons have gone to the mountains. The Fell one[2] believes that now is the time to corner them. War is coming." "How can you be so sure?" "I can't. I trust the Qi." They stood in silence.

"If he issues the army, we may all need a place to stay," explained Yia. Both women turned to take in the scenery. To the North, the Patal house sat nestled between the ancient oaks, the boughs of the trees softly grazing the adobe-tiled roof. Behind the house, the Northern section of the trail twisted off into the hills. To the South where the two Urumqi stood, the trail gave way from shaded leaves to dusty sand, where it would eventually cross the East Road. "This place would be ideal," nodded Mrs. Patal, taking the hint. Yia paused. "Can you call them?" she whispered quickly. The other woman looked down at the rosebush. "Long live the Urumqi."

The oak trees, the hills, the tiled roof faded from Mrs. Patal's mind. Her will crossed the rolling valley, making its way to the southern section of the West Road. Yia knew that the eldest generation of Urumqi would come. 'Seek refuge or perish.'

"What's our count so far, Mike?" boomed Steve Kanoka over the din of shovels, pick-axes, and pulleys. "Hundred tons, all City bound," replied Steve's colleague. "Think we'll hit the three hundred mark by sundown tonight?"

"Three hundred? That's major overtime for your buddies at tunnel seven," replied Mike skeptically. "I'll say what I always say, man; just get it done," ordered Steve. "Will do, boss."

Steve Kanoka turned to take in the vast expanse that was his rock quarry. Instead of operating all businesses directly, some types of industrial production such as mining and forestry were sanctioned to certain individuals by the Empire. This meant that all of Steve's workers did not choose to be miners; the job was chosen for them. In this respect, Steve knew that he was fortunate to possess one of the most desirable jobs in Uru. However, there was one thing undesirable about Steve Kanoka's job: his all too frequent meetings with the overseer. The overseer was a dwarflike man with a mean looking face, complete with dark, beady eyes that seemed to pierce one's will.

It was at this moment that such a man approached Steve from behind. "Mr. Kanoka?" It was clearly more of an accusation than a question. Steve swiveled slowly to face him. "Yes?" "By order of the Imperial court, I must revoke permission for you to run this quarry. A military and economic lockdown will soon be in effect. I suggest that you return home and await instructions." Steve was in shock. "As for the rest of you," continued the overseer, "don't stop until five hundred tons have been shipped to the..." "Five hundred? Are you crazy?" broke in Mike. Steve just looked at him sadly, knowing that his friend would not make it through the night.

All around Uru, the sanctioned bosses were sent home, the remaining workers forced to work overtime to prepare for the issuing of the army. Word soon spread to the Patal home. Yia's prediction was correct; war was coming. The waves of deathly dry tension that plagued the dusty streets of Uru were about to be released. The tension in Dan Carver's home had already broken. "You used to be a good person, dad!" shouted Dan with unthinkable rage. "You've taken my life's goal, my life's dream, and ripped it out of my hands just to make a stack of filthy coins! My friends could...my friends will die because of you...dad...you're not my dad...murderer!"

Deafening horns shattered the quiet of Imperial City. The gate guards fetched their whips. The beast keepers fastened the brazen collars to the defiant wolves. With another fanfare from the trumpeter, the three massive gates of the City groaned as they sluggishly opened. Sixteen abreast, the first legion of crimson soldiers marched from the central gate. Just behind the legion, Gorath stood on the deck of an abandoned shop, watching his masterpiece. Igni slinked toward him. "Guran say *my* men go first," he hissed. Gorath took one massive step closer to the now frightened Elite commander, the rotting wood creaking dangerously beneath his feet. "The Guran be not the master of this great Empire, oh ghoulish one. Me orders come directly from me Emperor," rumbled the giant. "Very well...this not over," rasped Igni.

Qur'shan stared up at the guard towers where the wolves pulled the great gates. When he first came to Imperial City, he was fascinated by them. After becoming good friends with one of the beast tenders, he had offered to accept two older wolves that were seen unfit to pull the gates. Because of the cramped quarters and malnutrition that ran rampant through the towers, he knew that with the proper care, the wolves had the potential to be just as strong as they once were. The first was an albino looking jackal with hardened, cream-colored fur. He was Qur'shan's first loyal companion. The other wolf was an old grandfather of the mountains with sharp grizzled fur and deadly fangs.

Glancing across the way, Qur'shan heard Igni's dissatisfaction with Gorath and his orders. "I think I have an idea," he said forcefully, getting the Elite leader's attention.

"I listen." "Go up towards the left passage, as if you were leaving the City, and veer left at the archway. A ways down, there's a drainage arc under the wall." "What? I don't know..." hissed the fiendish leader. "Alright...I'll show you..."

Aaron Brown and his Mandos cooked their meager midday meal over a miserable little fire in the drainage archway. Until forced to hide in his own City, Aaron had never taken stealth seriously. "Hey. Someone comes," scraped one of the Mandos. "In here," ordered Aaron. "And put out that fire!" As the Mandos watched from the door of an old housing complex, Aaron saw Igni carefully examine the drain. Aaron had never actually spoken to the Elite leader, but he had spent enough time around the Guran to know who he was. Another man appeared on the scene. He was far taller than Igni and he carried many of the same weapons that Aaron frequently used. "Through there," said the man. "You'll make it to the foothills long before the army reaches the Crossroads." Igni turned. "I want see you fight. You go with me." "Very well," said the man. "Always a pleasure to kill a sorcerer."

Chapter Nine-
Of Parents and Grandparents

The trip down the mountain seemed to take forever. There was no need to say aloud that tensions were running high. "Why do you care so much about her?" Even from Vicky, such a comment seemed unnecessarily rude and out of place. He had tried to explain to her that Jordan was going through a hard time and that she needed their support more than ever. He even ventured to remind her of how his minor disagreement with Aan had nearly destroyed the Urumqi. "The only real mistakes are the ones in which we fail to learn something!" he had tried to explain. But somehow, he knew that she would never understand. Things would be different once they reached the West Road; of this, Oro was certain. More than ever, Oro wondered if he would ever see Caliphia again. There was no time to say goodbye.

To Oro's right, Ja walked steadily down the steep, gravelly path. Oro's question broke the silence. "What did you mean when you said 'I am you'?" Ja turned suddenly. "I've never told anyone about my family." Oro wondered if there was any way to get Ja to say more. "You've told me lots of secrets, man. And all of them are *still* secrets." "Alright," Ja replied shakily.

"Remember after the Battle of the Temple when I told you that my parents were killed by the Empire?" Oro nodded. "Well that's not the whole truth. I don't actually know if my father is alive or dead. He was taken captive by Viron before I was born. Well at least that's what my mother told me." Ja paused. "When I was very little, the Empire raided my village and…they killed her." "They killed your mother?" asked Oro. "They killed everyone…well, there was one…"

he broke off. "Why are you asking me this, Oro? These things aren't meant to be known," he snapped. Oro wished he had just kept his mouth shut.

A ways behind them, Ava and Mandi were engaged in a much less serious conversation. "No way! You mean you're actually into Oro?" exclaimed Mandi. Ava looked at her long time friend sheepishly, choosing not to respond. "We've known him for almost seven years, and now you tell me...what about Slay?" "What about Slay?" repeated Ava. "Well it seemed like you two got along just fine," teased Mandi. "I was never that serious about him, though," Ava clarified. "What about you? Who are you serious about?" asked Ava, flipping the direction of their conversation. Mandi didn't answer right away. "Don't you love it that Ja is so much more friendly now?" "Wow, you and Ja, I would have never guessed," laughed Ava.

Most people in Uru could not remember the last time that the army had been summoned. Many thought it to be a formality rather than a military force, especially Aan's father, Mr. Huila. The officer who had released him from his position of agricultural boss at the local commune had mentioned something about a lockdown. As he trudged homeward toward the West Road, he heard whispers from the other farmers that the great purge of the Urumqi had begun. If this were the case, it would be crucial that he not be seen returning home. Ever since Viron's coming of age, no Urumqi was safe, not even in the cellars of their homes. He knew that Viron had the power to think like an Urumqi. For when his mind perceived the clay tiled roof resting between the oaks, he was at first wary of a trap.

The Huila home rests evenly between the Crossroads and the base of the mountain. Mr. Huila could just see the corner of the rooftop as he stepped from the dirt farm-trail onto the road. The rest of what he saw was what amazed him. Along the sides of the road, the crimson royal guard worked in pairs, digging multiple layers of heavily fortified trenches. Others carried crates full of weapons, some marked with a dangerous looking X. At the head of the pack, the metal clad Elite warriors oversaw the entire operation, directing both the trench diggers and the supply carriers, waving their spade-like swords in the air. As Mr. Huila neared his own home, he saw that his front porch had been torn up to make room for a trench.

"What's going on here?" he asked in the kindest tone possible. "Your property in way," rasped one of the warriors from under his metal faceplate. "This road not safe more. Find other place stay before boss Igni harms," he said, brandishing his sword. 'This has gotten out of hand,' thought Mr. Huila. Inside, he found his wife and daughter sitting nervously in the kitchen. "Time to go," he whispered.

Across Uru, the Urumqi received Mrs. Patal's telepathic message. Following in Mr. Huila's footsteps, the elder generation of Urumqi left their homes to seek refuge from Viron's army at the Patal home. Mr. Ridder was forced to leave his immaculately spotless kitchen and set out down the farm-trail. Mr. Marah and his son looked back one last time at the little house in the valley, the porch crumbling away. Mrs. Andora gathered her family from the craggy hills, barely avoiding the crimson troops.

Not all were as fortunate as the Huila family in this time of trial. From the dusty old flat in the Traditional quarters of the West side, Mr. Mitchel stared at his newly drawn map of Uru, thinking about his son. "Something has happened to Stan," he said, startling his wife. She had been sitting by the window, watching the crimson troops file past her home. It was at this moment that he snapped. "Those filthy Imperials will pay!" he screamed, tearing the map in half. Rushing out of the rickety front door, he swept his hand wildly in the air, causing six of the soldiers to double over. Blood squirted from their eyes, crusting in little pools on the dusty path. "I am special! No one can defeat me!"

Hearing the commotion from atop his grizzled wolf, an Elite commander rode quickly to the entrenchments further up the road to consult his superior. "Sir...we haves...an Urumqi elder," hissed the Elite commander. "Perfect," breathed Igni. "Take this," he said, handing the Elite commander one of the crates marked with an X. "Next to him, leave it on fire," cackled Igni. "You see what happen."

On that dusty path, Mr. Mitchel fought like one possessed. So focused on bringing death and destruction he was that he failed to see the Elite commander on wolf-back, carrying the box and an oil torch. The blast leveled the one room flat completely. The soldiers just stared in awe at the power that their Emperor commanded. Near Tib's Temple, a ripple of pain passed through Mr. Marah's thoughts. "One of us has perished," he said quietly to Mr. Lia, who walked sadly at his side. "Yes..."

The first to arrive at the Patal home was Mrs. Andora. After quickly greeting Mrs. Kanoka and Mrs. Patal, she proceeded out to the trail to set up what few belongings she had been able to carry with her. Next to arrive was Mr. Huila. "I never thought I'd say this, but you were right," he said quietly to Yia. She just nodded and massaged her chin. "We cannot hide from Viron; we must face him," he added, with a little more confidence. After the Huila family was settled in, more and more families arrived. Yia knew most of them, but not all. After hours of waiting, there were only three who had not yet come. As rugged looking and as fashionably late as always, Mr. Marah could be seen, slowly walking the road to the Patal house, Mr. Lia and young James at his side.

"It's been a long time," said Yia, giving him a quick hug. "I knew you'd come eventually," she laughed. "Speaking of which," grumbled Mr. Marah, "where is that Ridder fool?"

he asked, sliding his palm along the handle of young James' stone hammer. "Now, now," teased Mrs. Patal. "If we're going to do this, we must settle our differences." "Agreed," he scoffed.

Late that night, Mr. Ridder stumbled onto the Patal property. He hated moments like this. Before he had seen the soldiers, he had maintained the belief that *nothing* could force him back to his old Urumqi council. Somehow, all of that had changed.

"Oro says there are eighteen," whispered Yia to Mrs. Patal as she gazed up at the sky. "Only thirteen families have come," she replied. "The rest are dead," stated Yia.

Chapter Ten-
The Empire at War

Deep in the dungeons of the Imperial Palace, the greasy haired technician watched as his minions loaded the magical substance into the crates marked with an X. A capsule of the stuff was first given to him by the Guran, who claimed he had taken it from a rogue Mando looking to make a few coins. All the Guran had told him was that the stuff was sensitive to heat. Since then, his primary goal had been to carefully examine and test the small capsule to learn how to make more. Now, twenty crates a day were produced from the cheapest and simplest substances. He couldn't wait for the fighting to begin. 'They'll never know what hit 'em.'

A few floors above, the Guran sat with his favorite student on a cold stone bench. "You are strong now, Kira," he said slowly. The girl looked to her mentor in surprise. Never had she seen the Guran compliment one of his students. "Yes," she whispered. "Soon war will come," rasped the Guran. "Igni cannot possibly kill all of them. Besides, there are the elders as well." Kira knew that her mentor spoke of the Urumqi. "You know what must be done," he crackled, "...all of them are yours to command, now. When the time comes, take the apprentices and *end* this abomination." "For you, master," she said, nodding her head slightly.

"One more thing," coughed the Guran before Kira had a chance to stand. "Once the Urumqi are no more, only one threat remains." The Guran watched as his favorite student's eyes lit up. "Soon we will be stronger than the Emperor and Uru will be ours!"

A slow sadness had fallen over the Urumqi as they descended from the cliffs and crags. Every one of them knew that upon return, they would face a very different world. Oro trailed the rest of the group, talking quietly with Nom. Leading the way was Vicky, who had refused to talk to anyone since her argument with Oro. Just behind her, Jordan was pretending to be in on Vince and Jim's conversation. 'She's so alone,' thought Oro.

Aan was the first to see the trenches. They started just before his house, and ran parallel along the edges of the West Road. Wooden crates marked with red paint lined the road next to the ditches. "What are those?" blurted Jim, once it was apparent that no one was going to ask. "Don't get too close," warned Ryan. "I'll open one," said Seth. Vicky didn't care. She kept walking down the road. "Don't…Come back…" called out Jordan, but it was already too late. "Get back!" yelled Jim as he saw the metal clad warrior leap from the trench to torch the line of boxes. Jim knew what was inside of the crates. It was Dan's blaster powder.

The Urumqi towards the front of the group were blown violently backward. Oro raced towards them. His eyes locked on Jordan as the flames licked her unconscious body. He knew that Vicky was even further into the inferno, but that didn't matter. Racing towards his girl, Oro tore open his traveling pack and doused the flames with water. Blood dripped from Jordan Lia's right shoulder, which had been snagged by a sharp rock.

Those who had not been knocked unconscious soon found themselves face to face with scores of Elite warriors, many riding on wolf-back. Having been toward the back of the group, Wanda, Slay, and Zach formed a tight circle, as not to expose their backs to the Elite warrior's spade-like swords. Wanda's staff glowed eerily. The bright blue discharge of energy sent three of her opponents backward, their armor melting from the intensity of the strike.

Ava and Mandi adopted a similar strategy, jumping back to avoid the chaos of the swords only to leap forward and devastate the Elite fighters. Wendy struggled to pull Aan's unconscious body away from the ever growing mayhem. Tears in her eyes, she watched her boyfriend's only home burn to the ground. Since his battle with Derek, Nom's strength had only grown. Using a series of rolls to reach the wall of fire, a sweep of his hand pushed the flames away from his companions and toward the attacking warriors.

Ja had not yet acted. Seconds before the explosion, he had stealthily shifted behind a large oak tree. Thus he was the first to see the leader of the Elite enter the battle. The fighting…the fire…it reminded him too much of the Battle of the Temple. In his mind, he saw himself choking the Elite warrior on the rooftop of Tib's temple, forcing him to tell who had run. 'I was too late to save her!' his mind screamed.

Igni tripped. Well at first, it appeared so. But soon he realized that he was being dragged away from the battle by some supernatural force. Ja stepped out from behind the oak tree, his opponent steadily moving toward him. A flick of his wrist sent Igni's armor crumbling away. Igni couldn't breathe; he watched as the thin boy in front of him tightened his fist at his side. Qur'shan was not a second too late. Ja did not see the steel gauntlet as it smashed into the side of his scull. "Me thanks Qur'shan," hissed Igni, catching his breath.

Igni did not know that he had been followed. Upon seeing the Elite leader leave Imperial City, Aaron Brown and his group of Mandos had decided to follow him. As the seventeen rogue Mandos reached Aan's burning house, the crates of blaster powder continued to explode without warning. Aaron looked deep into the flames that barred the road. "Someone lives!" he called to his company. "Go! Help the others..." he ordered his group.

Aaron's specially crafted armor, backed by unyielding chain mail, was more than a match for the periodic explosions. Wading into the flames, he helped the struggling figure to safety. Her right arm, tightly gripping a long, jagged staff, was badly burned. Aaron's eyes moved upward to the girl's face. He knew exactly who she was: Vicky Marah. Her cold eyes stared back at him. Neither dared to speak.

Oro was able to stop the bleeding. A torn off piece of his jacket now held Jordan's shoulder. Her eyes opened to find Oro holding her, choking back tears. "I love you," she said impulsively, wrapping her arms tightly around him.

The tide was slowly turning. Distracted by the entrance of the Mandos, Igni and his warriors rushed into the battle, temporarily forgetting the Urumqi. Towards the outskirts of the battle, Ava and Mandi met up with Seth and Mac. "We can't cut 'em all down ourselves," panted Seth. "We need to awaken the others, even if it means rushing back in there," agreed Mac. "I...I think I can heal them," stammered Ava. "It's our only chance," concluded Seth.

Rushing forward with tremendous speed, Seth and Mac cut a gap in the line of oncoming attackers. Ava came across Aan's unconscious body first. Not knowing what to do, she tried to relax and let the Qi flow through her. The battle gave way to a sea of smoke. A slow sweep of her hand cleared the thick fog from Aan's body. Wendy watched from a distance, simultaneously beheading a warrior, as her boyfriend stood. She walked slowly over to Ava. "Thank you, and may the stars watch over you," said Wendy. Her guilt over Shelly's death had at last been lifted.

Ja awoke to find Mandi affectionately watching over him. Nom had succeeded in squelching most of the lingering flames. "You're welcome," scoffed Aaron, after waiting for Vicky's thanks, which he knew would never come. "Fall back!" hissed Igni at Qur'shan's urging. Vicky stumbled close to where Jordan lay with her arms still tightly locked around Oro. Her burnt right hand still gripped her long, jagged staff. She raised her weapon. Ja quickly rested his hand on her shoulder. "Anger is not the way," he said prophetically, ignoring Mandi for the moment.

Part Four- The Fall

Chapter One- The Urumqi Reunited

The Main Man was utterly overwhelmed. But he was not surprised. After the death of his predecessor, Nate Farelle, he knew it was only a matter of time before the violent clashes between the many factions of Uru would draw the Empire's gaze. As the leading information dealer of the East side Traditionals, he knew exactly whose fault this was. The Urumqi. He did not despise them...how could he? He simply admired their brotherhood and courage that had emerged after the Battle of the Temple. He knew they had the potential to stop the Imperial tyranny.

But none of this mattered, because he knew that his people, those people who counted on him to bring light to dark times, could never...would never understand what was truly at hand. Most believed the Urumqi to be a dying race. Some even thought them to be entirely extinct. Doubtlessly these rumors had been started by the Empire to crush any thought of opposition. So here's what he told them. "They have issued their armies for but one reason. They wish for us to join them. They are not just our rulers anymore; they have become a faction, a faction who wishes to absorb us, to destroy our livelihood, so that they can conquer all of Uru...absolutely." He told them this, because he knew that any mention of rebellion would be looked upon as foolish.

By telling his people that they must *defend*, he stood a chance of helping the Urumqi to crush Viron's evil reign.

"They march our streets as we speak!" exclaimed Banda, brandishing his jagged edged sword wildly in the air. "What can I do?" sighed the Big Man, with a hint of despair in his voice. "Those two-faced Urumqi destroyed everything that I worked to build. And now...now that the Empire itself is knocking on my front door, I have no one to turn to besides them." Banda looked at his master questioningly. "Do you regret my decision when I told them that a loan would be foolish?" "No, you did the right thing. I have faith, Banda, that we are not alone. Every Contemporary family is facing the same thing that I am. Together, we will find a way."

In his boxlike flat near the coast, Max Toko talked with his long time friend, Dave Datsun. "It's all over, man. We can't offer protection from Imperial soldiers," rumbled Max angrily. "It's not over until we give up," replied Dave with a hint of a smile. Max just looked back at him questioningly. "It isn't too late to rally the Agents and join the Urumqi," he said. Silence. "I'm doing it for dad," said Dave with finality. "Are you in?" Max looked around at the broken pictures, at the peeling paper on the walls. It wasn't much, but it was home. "They'll never know what hit 'em," said Max, widening his silly grin.

And so things were, when the band of seventeen Urumqi and fifteen Agents walked the deserted valleys of Uru in secret, behind the East Road, journeying to the Patal house, the ancient center of resolve. When the Urumqi first arrived at the old wooden door, little was said. Most found their families, hoping to find some measure of comfort in this trying time. Those who were alone simply chose a place on the ground, unrolled the remainder of their possessions, and waited. The Mandos never asked to camp behind the safety of the house. They dug meager trenches just off of the road and tried to get some rest.

Inside the wilting home, things went on as usual. No one saw Nom. Oro looked around inquisitively, waiting for someone to say something…to say anything. Even Yia seemed detached, in a way that Oro had never seen her before. On the third day, Oro realized what was happening. The fell poison with which Derek Drake had tried to intoxicate his friends was at work among his elders. He watched as Mr. Ridder and Mr. Marah exchanged hateful looks. He saw the very same look in Mr. Huila's eye that he had seen in Aan's, that night at the Temple so long ago. He knew that he was the only person who stood a chance of making a difference.

Well, not the only person. There was one other who could solve this…who could fix it… But she was no longer among the living.

You set me free
To live my life
You became my reason to
Survive the great divide
You set me FREE

The wind blew, rustling the leaves around the oak trees. "What are we going to do, huh?" shouted Oro a bit too loudly in the Urumqi camp. "Is this our strategy? To sit here and hide until Viron finds us?" He had succeeded in getting almost everyone's attention now. "This isn't a plan! You're a bunch of cowards who don't want to confront each other." He waited to see who understood. "I can see the same rift in all of you that I experienced myself. You would all be foolish to turn away from the lesson that I can show you." He glanced around at his friends, hoping someone would offer their support. Consumed by the pressure of being with their families, no one did. "Vicky!" called out Oro suddenly. "You know what I mean, right? You used to think that my friends and I were stubborn, condescending snobs. But now you've realized that we're all in this together, right?"

Vicky just stared back at Oro, her father's gaze piercing the flesh on the back of her neck. "I don't know what you're talking about, Oro," she shouted, glancing hopefully behind her. "You and your 'friends' are slimy snobs! We should have killed Ridder when we had the chance!" Oro was dumbstruck. Vicky turned her head round to look at her dad, as if expecting some kind of praise. Mr. Ridder pointed at Yia with rage. "I told you not to let *them* stay here!" he spat. Jordan Lia looked at her best friend, tears in her eyes. "You're wrong, Vicky," she said quietly. "I've become a part of the family, the Urumqi family, now. Why can't you?" Impulsively, she ran to Oro and embraced him. "Countless times, you've done what none of us could. I will follow you," she whispered.

"The young ones are right; that much I know," said Yia. "There's too much hate, too many secrets, too much tension among us. If we refuse to stand united, we will fall. Of this much I am certain." Her words seemed to cast a spell on the group. Yia walked slowly over to Vicky. "You didn't really mean what you said, did you dear?" she asked kindly. Vicky stared back at her coldly. "Just because your father is at odds with Mr. Ridder doesn't mean you have to be." Nobody thought that Vicky would answer. But she did. "If you can't stand by your family...what else is there?" she cried out sharply. "There is the Qi," whispered Yia.

Stepping back, Yia Kanoka continued her talk. "What you say isn't true, dear. Just look at Oro. His immediate family...his parents...are not Urumqi. Yet he still finds the courage within himself to stand and address you. Will you not listen to what he says?" A quiet murmur rose from the onlookers. Never before had the elders heard of an Urumqi born alone, without an Urumqi parent. "The Kanoka family is strong indeed," called out Mr. Huila above the chatter.

"Forgive him, friend," he said, resting his old hand on Mr. Ridder's shoulder. Ryan looked at his father. "Do it, dad…" Mr. Ridder nodded his head.

Chapter Two-
The Forming of a Plan

"At last, we have learned to forgive," chuckled Yia with a wry smile. "As Oro pointed out, we cannot just sit here," repeated Aan. "We *must* come up with some kind of plan. There must be some vulnerability created by the issuing of this wretched army. We need to find it." "Say no more," came a chilling voice from across the yard. Aaron Brown approached quickly. "Unbelievable! How do we know he isn't a traitor?" shouted Mr. Marah before anyone could explain. "Yeah, get him dad!" shouted young James, copying his father. Vicky looked forlornly at her family, all confidence lost. If she didn't stop her family, she knew that Oro's lunatic of a grandmother would try to teach her another pointless lesson. But if she did...her mind flashed back to the explosion, to the fire, to Aaron's metal clad arms pulling her from the cursed flames. Her conscious was utterly distraught. 'I don't need him. He didn't save me...' "Kill him, dad," she said.

Nom waved his staff, pushing Mr. Marah off his feet. "Don't you understand? If it wasn't for him, your own daughter would be dead. Why this untamed hatred? Over the years, what has it gained you?" Mr. Marah stood dangerously. "Don't you ever touch me..." "No," said Nom, keeping him in check. "My power comes from nothing save my experience. You know I'm right."

"Anyway," said Aaron, breaking the tension, "what I know is that the entire red army was scheduled to move out in order to occupy all of Uru while you were away. Imperial City is now empty. They are all hunting for you. My men reported this to me last night." "Then this is our opportunity to take the City," concluded Nom. "It's going to be next to impossible to get inside if the City is locked down, which it must be, since its standing army is gone. And even if we did get inside, how many of us can fight Guranqi? Who can battle the Emperor?" asked Jim. "Well I don't know, but I do know that we'll need a much larger group if we plan on taking the city," said Wanda.

"It seems to me that there are many others in Uru who are doing the same thing as you," mentioned Aaron, again offering his advice. "Mostly the Traditionals' information dealers and wealthy Contemporaries, if I had to say, are staying in groups to spread the word without alerting the army. There's a reason that they told everyone to go home, and they know it." "We'll have to ask for their help," said Jim. The others stared at him. Nobody had ever heard of Jim accepting help, let alone asking for it. "Stan knew the streets better than anyone, but he's gone now, and I must follow in his footsteps. I can find the Main Man." "I'm with you," said Vince. "Ryan and I can go to the Contemporaries," offered Wanda. "Nom and I will find Max and the rest of the Agents," called out Mac. "And we're already here; that wasn't so hard, was it?" joked Aaron.

"I must also leave," boomed Ja, just after the others began to stir. "No, we can't afford to lose anyone else," answered Aan, without even asking why. "It wasn't a question," said Ja darkly. "I must also leave."

"There, good as new," wheezed the Imperial Tech, attaching the final brace to Derek's arm. The journey back to the City had been a painful one. The duel with Nom had left him weakened. The pain never ceased. Even more painful was the news that the ambush at the foot of the mountains had failed. All forms of stealth and trickery had been exhausted. Derek knew that the only way to defeat the Urumqi was by sheer force. He knew that the Urumqi would not simply sit and wait. He knew that they would come for him.

"You have failed Igni," stated Viron. "Hmm yess, but Igni know for sure that we killed one Urumqiss…" "Do not try to mitigate your failure with one tiny triumph. There should have been eighteen casualties, not one!" Igni cowered in fear. "Go, send out more scouts, take more wolves if you need them, just find those Urumqi and kill them before my patience runs out!" Igni slinked away, the door closing dangerously close behind him. "Don't mind him," cackled the Guran, slipping out of nowhere to face Igni. "I know that he relies on you. It is you who will end this war, I foresee." "Hmm" "The Emperor is weak; do as I say and you will become a great hero."

Qur'shan stood above the drainage arc, looking down at a charred spot in the rock gully. He remembered seeing, just three days before, a pile of hot ashes when he had first shown the place to Igni. It was that day that he had fought a rogue group of Mandos, who had somehow known about the ambush at the foothills. If this was the case, he knew it was possible that these Mandos had been camping in the City, thus explaining the ashes. He knew that these Mandos were allied with the Urumqi, and that they could easily enter the City unnoticed. Using metal anchors and razor wire, he formed a makeshift net across the tunnel.

Because of his parents' special agreement with the Empire, Dan Carver's residence had been left untouched. He had heard rumors of a great Urumqi ambush, and he hoped that his invention had not been used against his friends. His friends. This wasn't the first time that he had sat alone in his room thinking about his friends. And the last time, his failure to act had resulted in the loss of a life. Grabbing two blasters and as many powder capsules as he could carry, he set out down the East Road. He didn't know where he was going, but anywhere was better than his room.

The Coast was a place of incessant change. It is the place where He first came. Yet it is the place where the Empire has had the least control. What was left of the free market remained near the waterfront. Rebels of all kinds sought refuge among the many peers and docks, many of which now littered the beach, their wooden supports decaying. And this is where the Urumqi chose to send…to rally the freedom fighters of Uru. Traditionals and Contemporaries alike left their homes in secret to join as one in the fight against oppression.

Oro saw Vicky walking alone on the trail. He quickened his pace to catch up to her. He didn't know what he was going to say. She had humiliated him in front of everyone he knew. She had made him, Oro Kanoka, look like a fool. "Hey there," he said, trying not to sound too negative. "Don't lecture me, Oro," she said. "Lecture? Lecture you? Oh don't worry; I'm not going to lecture you. I'm finished trying to fix all your problems. You don't trust the Urumqi, you don't trust my friends, and worst of all, you don't trust me. If all you can trust is your pathetic quarreling family, then go! Let us do our job." "I don't need you, Oro. You're becoming just like them!" "Everything is *them* with you, Vicky. Nothing is ever *we*. It's just *you* and *them*. But I guess you have no problem with that." He turned away from her. He walked away.

I tried to be perfect
But nothing was worth it
I don't believe it makes me real
I thought it'd be easy
But no one believes me
I meant all the things that I said
If you believe it's in my soul
I'd say all the words that I know
Just to see if it would show
That I'm trying to let you know
That I'm better off on my own

Chapter Three- A Gathering

It took a full day for everyone to travel to the coast. When Oro finally arrived, he was overcome by sadness. Looking across the crowd, he saw faces, faces of people who had left their homes, their belongings, their lifestyles, simply because they believed in the message of the Urumqi. He saw the Main Man and the Big Man sitting together on an overturned crate. He saw Aaron point respectfully at Max and Dave. And right in front of him stood Ja Kahn, with a young boy standing beside him. "The only survivor of the Empire's raid on my village…my…my son," Ja said quietly to Oro. Oro didn't know what to say.

"Attention everyone," boomed Mr. Huila, using the Qi to increase the volume of his voice. "I do not know how much time we have until the Empire will notice our absence. If we are to take the City before the army's return, we must quickly come up with a plan. We have no superior weapons to give you, so our tactic must be to overwhelm. I believe that once we are inside the City, other men trapped within will join our cause. From there, we can hope to lay siege to the palace while the Urumqi find a way inside.

"However, entering the City will not be easy. Although the army uses the central gate, they do not typically travel in the valley just in front. They march around the cliffs, toward the West Road. If we can reach this central valley undetected," he said, pointing to Mr. Ridder who was creating a rough map in the sand with his staff, "then we have a chance of rushing the central gate…" He trailed off as Aaron tapped him on the shoulder. "The gates are opened by cylindrical winches atop the guard towers on either side," Mr Huila continued, using Aaron's knowledge to give his audience a more detailed explanation. "Our first priority should be to find a way into the towers in order to open the gate." He couldn't tell if anyone understood. "Try to get into groups; the best way to fight is to stick together."

Turning to his fellow Urumqi, Mr. Huila joined the group in discussing more specific plans. "Only problem I can see is that if we can't get the gates open, we're stuck," pointed out Mr. Ridder. "We have to have the entire front of the City surrounded; there is no other way," explained Mr. Lia. "If we attack one gate, they'll just fortify that one three times as much." "Exactly," said Yia softly. "What?" he said. "If we trick them into thinking that we are staging a single-front assault, it will leave the other gates free of guards. I suggest that we allow our children to split off from the main group and enter through the side gates…" "Are you sure it's worth risking their lives?" asked Mrs. Andora hysterically. "They are strong," said Yia. "They are the heroes, not we."

Oro overheard what his grandmother had said. And he knew it would be up to him to divide the group in two. After explaining the plan to the others, he attempted to create two squads within the group of seventeen. "Aan and I can lead the assault, one of us on each side. Our goal will be to meet in the middle to enter the palace. Ryan, Wanda, since both of you are good leaders, you two should split up as well." Oro was surprised to see Ryan make the first move, stepping closer to him. "Now for the rest of you," continued Oro, "who do you work best with? Who do you want by your side during battle? Remember, we need equal numbers on each side." Of course, Wendy had already found her place at Aan's side. Seth, Slay, and Zach also stepped towards Aan. In turn, Ava and Mandi went to Oro. "He's gonna need all the help he can get," said Ja quietly to Oro. Turning to Aan, he said louder "my son stays with me." Balancing the numbers, Nom and Mac joined Oro. Looking sadly back at Vicky, Jordan went to Oro, followed by Vince. Jim reluctantly stepped towards Aan, never failing to look like a rebel. And Vicky...Vicky just stood there. "Do what you want," scoffed Oro.

"Ho, Emperor," called Gorath, trying to squeeze through the metal door of the throne room. "What news have you for me?" asked Viron. "People are...leaving, sir, most quietly, as if avoiding my men...what shall I do?" The Emperor stood slowly and walked up to Gorath. The Commander and Chief shook with fear. "Do *not* let them reach the City," boomed Viron. "When they attack, surround them and kill them."

"I find there is very little need for walking these days," whispered the Guran as he floated next to Kira down the City's thoroughfare. "That is my advice to you, young one. Feelings are not just internal; they create an aura about you. Learn to control this aura and you can achieve mastery of the Qi." Kira attempted to lift herself from the ground. After a few moments of shaking, she steadied herself and turned to her master. "I have spoken with the others. We will spread out to cover the whole City. What of you, master?" The old man paused and looked down at his metal crutch. "There is someone I must face." With that, he left Kira's side and headed toward the central gate.

The Urumqi elders set out first. There were fourteen of them. All marched for war save one, Nom's grandmother, who had chosen an alternative. "I will go to Tib's temple to meditate," she had said to Yia the night before. "Only two places have been innately interwoven with the Qi. Destroying the palace is not a physical task, but it is not impossible." Yia looked at her wisest friend. "I have faith...But what of the chest?" "It will come when the time is right," she had answered.

Next came the Agents and Mandos, many of them checking their equipment packs and sharpening their weapons. A few of them had forged metal arrows, choosing to rely on their accuracy rather than their combat skills. Behind them came the two parties of Urumqi led by Aan Huila and Oro Kanoka. Looking to those behind them, they attempted to sort the masses of Traditionals and Contemporaries based on the types of weapons they carried. Those bearing longbows, crossbows, or throwing weapons were directed to the sides of the group to hide in the hills on each side of the valley. Those with swords, knives, axes, hammers, spears, and clubs were tentatively organized into rows just behind the Urumqi. Some of them had no weapons at all. Most were able to scavenge from the surroundings, using rock, straw, and pieces of wood to construct unique weapons. A few of the bolder men had asked the Mandos for razor wire, which they wrapped around long pieces of wood to make their clubs more deadly. Amidst the chaos of the march, no one noticed two more people enter the pack. One carried a long tube and a backpack; the other carried nothing but an iron hammer.

'Everything is in motion,' mused the Guran. His wrinkled hand opened the small, single-man door just left of the towering central gate. Igni's men had regrouped, and were patrolling the length of the wall. Gorath had ordered the entire Imperial Army to return to the West Road, just South of the City, where they would be concealed by the rocky hills. The Guran stepped forth from Imperial City. His crutch foot sunk deeply into the mud. His good hand loosely griped his oldest weapon, a thin sword with a slightly bent hilt, crafted for a single fist. Adopting his fake limp, he hobbled toward the column of attackers.

"Say, I remember you," said young James Marah, tapping Max Toko. "You pretty much saved my life from those Mandos." Max turned round to look at him. "What up, man?" called out Max. "War. Anyway, you think it would be alright if I join you on the front lines? I really ought to see some action and I'm good with a hammer," said James.

"You seem confident," noted Max, "sure, why not. Take up a spot next to me here."

"Okay, do we all know what we're doing?" asked Aan for the hundredth time. "Yes, yes," grumbled Slay, "your group goes left, Oro's goes right. We stick to the hills until we're completely out of sight. Then, we rush in to attack the side gates, but only when the diversion has drawn the defenders away." "Yes," said Aan with finality.

By the time the Urumqi elders were close enough to see the outline of the walled City, the sun was already low in the sky. The marsh-like valley turned cool. A layer of fog had ominously floated in from the East, obstructing what lie ahead. "We must be nearly to the gate…but the whole City looks dark," whispered Mr. Huila to Yia. "Shall we try to light torches?" asked Mrs. Andora. "No!" hissed Mr. Marah, who was leading the group. "Something lurks in the shadow."

Chapter Four-
The Battle Begins

"Now," hissed Igni from atop the wall. The tinder men crept to the torches. All at once, the wall erupted in flames, shedding light upon the Urumqi. "Well...what have we here?" cackled the Guran, stepping forward to immerse himself in the firelight. "No!" gasped Mr. Marah upon recognizing the old man. "I can't do this. I won't face him," he cried, losing control. The Guran loosely raised an empty hand. In a mere instant, the old man's face contorted; his hand shot rigid. Mr. Marah was cast into the air, landing in a muddy heap on the wet earth. "You're pathetic. Why won't you face me?" rasped the Guran. "I have no choice." Mr. Marah's voice was muffled. The Guran leaned closer, and failed to notice the perfectly shaped tree branch soar overhead and land firmly into Mr. Marah's hand. "Auhhh," he grunted, knocking the Guran away with a devastating blow. "Now! To the wall!" hollered Mr. Huila to the others.

Yia was quickest to act. She waved her staff in an arc overhead. A silvery powder floated down over her, casting a shadow on her physical presence. Although, in her guise, her strides were slow, she made her way to the single door from which the Guran had exited the City. Slipping in quickly before the arrival of Igni's guards, she silently crept through the City, taking in all that she could.

The archers on both sides of the valley opened fire upon the wall. The wooden splints had little effect on the guards' jagged armor. "Now," hissed Igni to one of the torch bearers; the tinder man pulled out a burning piece of wood from the flaming bowl and hurled it from the top of the wall in the direction of the West Road. Those archers close enough to the firelight cried out, for the first time noticing the lines of crimson. A thousand Imperial Troops had been hiding in the darkness of the road, waiting to march forth. "Advance," called out a general. The legions filed forward, sliding their swords from their scabbards.

"This isn't going to work. Look at all those troops," shouted Dave above the din of the battle. "Quickly, come with me!" called out Aaron. After making sure that the others would follow, he began sprinting toward the drainage arc that he knew was just ahead. The four warriors reached the small pipe unseen by the crimson troops, who were preoccupied with the masses of Traditionals pouring over the hills, attempting a sudden flank. "We go in here," said Aaron. He laid himself down, crawling feet first into the pipe. "I'll go next," said James. "We're right behind you," called Max. Though there was no light coming from the City, Aaron knew that he was almost inside. Then, he stopped. Something was blocking the way. Something was caught around his ankle. Attempting to focus his eyes, the shadowy outline of razor wire came into view. Just as he was about to holler back to the others, he felt himself being yanked through the tunnel.

Seeing the Urumqi momentarily pause, two Agents with long cables rushed forward in a quick attempt to scale the wall. Several Elites leapt from the towers, their spade-like swords slashing wildly as they fell through the air. "This isn't going to work...they're all going to be slaughtered," said Mr. Ridder, referring to the Agents. "All Agents and Mandos, get to the right side of the valley and help the Traditionals," boomed Mr. Huila. He knew that if the soldiers were to advance any further, their position at the front gate would be compromised. Ushering the Urumqi forward, he prepared for the taking of the wall. "Even with those guards up there, there has to be a way for us to reach those towers," pondered Mrs. Andora. "The wall is old," said Mrs. Bera quietly. "What?" growled Mr. Ridder angrily. "It is old," she said.

Waving her hand, she loosened a few bricks from the outer layer. A second sweep of her hand caused them to line up in a stair step fashion.

The Guran watched the muddy earth sail under him. But he was determined not to land in the filth that he himself had created. He retained his aura, and floated eerily to the ground. He looked back the way he had been struck and saw Mr. Marah steadily marching toward him. "Fool," he spat, "how many more lessons must I teach you before you understand!" Mr. Marah did not break stride. "You did this to me…You hunted my family all those years…it was you. I knew it was you!" He tried to face his enemy, but the will to look away was stronger. Blindly, he swept his tree branch in a wide arc. The Guran parried it easily and twisted his wrist around with a dark speed, cutting into Mr. Marah's leg.

Exactly according to plan, Aan's party of Urumqi began their sprint towards the left side of the city. "Quickly, let's get the gates open!" said Aan. "I got it," said Ja. He reached upward and peeled a long strip of steel from the face of the gate, leaving the lower edge attached to the wood. "Hold this down," he said to Slay, handing over the bent piece of metal, whose bottom was still tightly anchored to the wall. Ja jumped on top of the strip. "Let it go," he said suddenly to Slay. The tension in the strip was enough to propel him to the top of the wall. Unseen, he cut the wires that held the gate in place, allowing one of the massive doors to swing awkwardly inward.

It didn't take long for the guards to realize what the Urumqi were doing. The stone stairs that the Urumqi were forging from the broken pieces of wall had nearly reached the top. "Fuel," hissed Igni. The guard next to him stared incredulously as the Elite leader moved a crate quickly through the torch fire before tossing it down the makeshift stairs. Seconds after the wooden crate left Igni's hands, it exploded into a shower of flames.

Oro's group had had to move even faster than Aan's to reach the right gate in time. Had they gone any slower, the scores of crimson guards would have closed the gap between the rocky hills and the City's wall. "No time to spare," said Vince quickly, motioning for the others to get back. He raised both hands in front of him, power crackling around his fingertips. All at once, he released his stream of energy toward the gate, causing one side to collapse inward from the overpowering force.

Although a large chunk had been torn away from Mr. Marah's calf, he did not cry out in pain. The Guran simply stood over him, cackling loudly. "You forget you are no different than I," he laughed. "Just as that age old duel long ago claimed my foot, in your flight I claimed yours!" A wave of the Guran's gnarled hand caused the remainder of Mr. Marah's wooden crutch to splinter away and burst into flames. "You were always good at walking," taunted the Guran. "You managed to walk away from me…a feat I once considered impossible. You turned away from the dark power I once gladly offered to you." He paused to drag Mr. Marah's body through the mud, closer to him, so that he might be forced to look the old man in the eye. "But look at you now…fool…you returned, and now you find nothing but pain and death. You are broken now, James. Here I will leave you to die." The old man began to float away. "I would kill you myself…but it seems to me that your friends are much more…dynamic targets."

A horn sounded from among the ranks of crimson troops. "Archers, prepare to fire! Soldiers, forward now! Close the gap," commanded a nearby general. Behind the thickening columns of troops, the once quiet archers opened fire upon the hillside. "We won't be able to hold this position long," said an Agent to a Mando who was fighting alongside him. "Then call for a retreat," he answered awkwardly. "To whom? I don't know where Max has gone…" "The Main Man," called out the Mando, pointing to the foot of the hill.

The Agent, fearing for his life, ran desperately towards the Main Man. "We can't hold the flank," he burst out. "Call for a retreat." "I can't," grumbled the Main Man. "I just spoke with the Urumqi and they say we must hold that position…"

Those closest to the dreaded corner began to fall back. The Traditional archers who lined the hilltop recoiled; volleys of arrows from the crimson archers cut down the stragglers. The bulk of the army groaned as the general's orders were made possible. The crimson troops eased forward, slowly narrowing the space between the hills and the City's wall.

"This isn't working!" boomed Mr. Huila over the shouts of the battle. More fiery crates continued to pound them from above. More Elite fighters were jumping down from the wall, somehow recovering quickly from the fall. Through the mess of bricks that the Urumqi had failed to use, the wolves from the guard towers made their way down from the wall, sinking their yellow teeth into anything not covered by metal. "We've got to think of something before we lose our entire army!" agreed Mr. Ridder. Just then, a large brick landed sloppily in the mud next to him. He looked up. With wooden beams from the top of the gate, some of the Elites had thrown together a catapult and were hurling the loose bricks downward.

Towards the back of the miscellaneous group of rabbles that was the Traditional army, the boy with the backpack looked around hopelessly. His unfocused gaze suddenly steadied on one man. The man looked weary. At his side, he carried a well crafted hammer. "Excuse me, sir, I need to get to the front lines." The man stared back at the boy wide eyed. "Are you okay, son? If you go to the front lines, you'll die." "Better me than my friends," replied the boy. "Now can you help me?" "I suppose."

Chapter Five-
A Lost Cause

Aaron felt himself being pulled through the drainage arc by his legs. Someone on the other side had seen him. "Go back!" he shouted to James just before his head left the pipe. Aaron looked up. He saw the man who had dragged him by the ankle and pulled the razor wire off his boot. The man appeared to be another Mando. "Who are you?" asked Aaron boldly. The other man responded with a quick chuckle. "You've got quite an attitude for a man whose been dragged from a sewage pipe." Aaron stared coldly back at the man, as if waiting for him to just answer the question. "I'm Qur'shan," said the man after a long pause. "And you are the Mando who so triumphantly foiled the Urumqi ambush." "True," said Aaron coolly. "And unless you want a repeat incident, you better just give up now." Aaron looked Qur'shan dead in the eye. He couldn't help but feel a sense of familiarity.

At Qur'shan's side rested a steel spiked ball, chained to a club-like handle. Lifting the unusual weapon with ease, he swung the ball toward Aaron, almost grazing his armor. "You can't frighten me," scraped Aaron, his voice slipping into its lowest key. Aaron Brown flicked out his scimitar and lunged toward his opponent. Blow after blow from the thin, flattened weapon caused Qur'shan to waver. But an opportunity arose. Underestimating the depth of his slash, Aaron's scimitar collided awkwardly with the club-like handle of Qur'shan's weapon. The other Mando retaliated, flipping the long handle in a sweeping motion. The blow caused Aaron to stumble out of his weapon's meager range. Before the massive collision, the whooshing sound of the spiked ball could be heard as it hurtled through the air. The pain was unlike any other that Aaron had ever known. It was as if his entire arm was dead, burnt off, cauterized out of its socket. Qur'shan stood over him. "Next time, don't be so quick to speak."

At first, Aan was surprised to find the streets deserted. Sad looking people cowered in their homes. Some hid their faces as the party of Urumqi walked by. Others looked upon them with admiration, as if they had been graced by some strange and extraordinary power. One old man eased open his rusty front door. "You've come to save us! Bless you!" he garbled with much enthusiasm. Ja's son approached the man. "May the stars watch over you," he said earnestly. The others looked at Ja incredulously. He just smiled, and nodded in approval.

"Look! Someone comes," growled Seth. A thin hooded figure approached the Urumqi, emerging from a cloud of rusty rotten dust. "Urumqi," she said. Her voice was high, bordering on unnatural. The word seemed to linger in the thick air, as if it had been shouted by a climber in the depths of an underground labyrinth. As the figure moved closer, so did the omnipresent aura of some twisted evil. When the dust settled, it became evident that the figure was not walking; *she* was not walking. She raised a wiry arm above her head. Eight Guranqi emerged from the rubble that bordered the road. Aan's eyes glanced at the row of enemies, and then in the direction of the City's front gate. "We have to keep moving," said Aan slowly. His intent was betrayed by his voice; the group would need to split up if they were to reach the palace in time.

Seth looked to his left and then to his right, making eye contact with Slay and Zach. "We can take them," he called out with confidence. Seth did not notice her. She floated eerily behind her eight defenders. Her eyes were drawn to Vicky, whose head drooped sadly downward. She clenched her fist and Vicky jerked awkwardly toward her. Their cold eyes locked. "I am Kira, and you will be the first to die," she sung. Kira's pale arms reached slowly upward, peeling off her hood. All at once, her physical aura vanished, and her black boots touched the ground. Her stance was unnaturally wide; she looked twisted, subhuman. "Wh-why me," stammered Vicky. It had taken her a few moments to regain her composure. "Because in you, there is much hate," whispered Kira.

Vicky's mind began to run rampant. She saw herself with Oro that night at the valley. She saw her bloodthirsty accusations against Aaron at Nom's. And she saw everything in between. "Yes, there is much hate," she repeated darkly. The blow from her long, jagged staff was too quick for Kira to react. It knocked her backward, but not as far as Vicky had thought. The hit would have killed…should have killed any living thing. Yet Kira stood unscathed. No blood dripped from her person. Her garments did not catch fire. Her pale skin did not melt away. Vicky's mind returned to the base of the mountains. The explosion had come out of nowhere; she had used her staff to blast the earth around her upward, covering herself from the intense heat. But her arm had not been covered. She remembered crying out as the flames licked at her skin. 'Now you will burn!'

Red fire shot from the end of Vicky's staff. Kira raised a gaunt hand. Upon reaching her palm, the fire swirled around her and then diminished. "You are foolish young girl," cooed Kira. "You cannot use anger against me. Your hate can give you no power." A double bladed sword appeared next to Kira. She had used the Qi to conceal her weapon. "Now you will die."

The five remaining Urumqi continued down the dusty street, now at a quick jog. They were almost to the palace. Aan heard cries of pain behind him. He felt responsible for the others, but he knew that the plan must not be abandoned.

"Wait," cried out Jim suddenly. He looked menacingly down a side street. A group of five men emerged from an old building and strode quickly down the street. "I must confront him," said Jim. "But..." interrupted Aan. "I must go," said Jim. He raced off down the side street in the direction that the five men had gone.

Four of the men were dressed in red. The fifth was a dwarflike man who looked out of place among the others. "Dad!" called out Jim. The short man turned around, and upon seeing Jim, he motioned for his guards to follow him. The overseer approached his son. "What are you doing here, Jim?" he blurted out. Jim paused. He really didn't have an answer. The overseer was not Jim's father and Jim was not his son. The overseer had never liked Jim, always leaving him to fend for himself. "I am one of them," said Jim finally. "I am an Urumqi." The overseer's beady eyes widened with disbelief. "I'm giving you one last chance, dad. Give up this campaign. Give up the Empire before it collapses and you fall down with it." The tone of his voice sounded more threatening than he had meant it to. Two Guranqi burst forth from a nearby storefront. Jim turned to face them. "Let us go," said the overseer to his guards.

Oro was surprised by what he saw as he walked through the City. But at the same time, he was not. He had always pictured the City folk to be rich beyond belief. But then again, he knew of the Empire's evil firsthand. Dusty faced people hid in their little wooden homes, shaking with each explosion from the front gate. He wanted to help them, to free them somehow. But his task was clear. He must meet up with Aan at the palace gates.

"Hush," whispered Ava suddenly. The others paused. "War drums," said Vince. "It's too fast to be a battle march..." concluded Ryan. A cloud of dust stirred on the road. The quaking came closer. "Look out!" shouted Nom. The nine Urumqi dived to the side of the road as the hulking form of

Gorath came charging toward them. Catching his breath, the Commander and Chief turned to face them. "Leave me'City NOW!" he bellowed. Nom glanced quickly at the others, indicating for them to leave him behind. He turned to face the giant. "Now…," he began slowly, "why exactly is it that you wish for my friends and I to leave this City?"

Gorath stared back at Nom, puzzled at being asked a simple question. "Because you're here to do harm to the Empire, and I can't let yah do that, now can I." Nom stepped closer, making no pretense of hostility. "And why is it that you care so deeply about the fate of the Empire?" An amount of time passed. It was obvious that Gorath did not have an answer. "Do not beguile me with your mystic trickery. Leave NOW!" he boomed. "I'm afraid I cannot do that," called out Nom, a hint of power in his voice. "Then I suppose I must force yah," growled Gorath. In his right hand rested a dull, squared off sword almost twice as tall as Nom.

Charging once again, Gorath swung wildly at Nom, all of his blows missing their target by a minute amount. "You are a good fighter," said Nom. "But you are too slow to ever stop me. Join us; we could use a man like you." The speech made Gorath even more irate. His blows became so quick that Nom was forced under the giant's legs. Seizing the opportunity, Gorath heaved his sword backward, its corner catching Nom's back. Blood caked in the dusty street. "You are not invincible," grumbled Gorath as he prepared for a finishing blow.

Not far from where the two fought, the other eight Urumqi jogged onward. Oro had a gut feeling that Aan was waiting for him. Just as he was about to break out into a sprint, Mac stopped him. "More troops ahead," he said, peering through the sheets of dust. "To the side of the road," called out Ryan. The Urumqi sought shelter among the broken splints of scrapped wood and metal, the remnants of what was once a clothing store. Old jackets and overcoats laid trampled into the mud. On the road, the troops broke into a jog, seeing Nom and Gorath just ahead. "It will take at least three of us to stop them," breathed Vince. Unnoticed by the others, Mac climbed nimbly to what was left of the second floor. In a single sweeping motion, he leapt from the building, landing in the midst of the frenzied troops. His first blow instantly beheaded the front most crimson soldier.

"We'll go," said Ava, nodding to Mandi. She looked Oro in the eye. He stopped for a moment. His mind raced backward, back to when the only thing he had to worry about was making it to Temple on time, back when the slightest smile from Ava had been enough to lift the darkness from any day. He stopped again. Looking back at her, he realized that the latter was still true. With renewed faith, he led the remainder of the group down the road. Almost at a run now they traveled, fearing that any further impediment of their progress would result in absolute failure. For this reason, it was not until the danger grew close that Oro heard the growls. Two wolves sprinted toward him from behind. The larger of the two was nearly upon them, bearing its fangs in anticipation of a meal. It lashed out, its claws slashing against Jordan's ankle. She tumbled to the ground, her hands sliding through the dust. "Oro!" she cried out sharply.

But he did not waver, he could not waver. Oro Kanoka, Ryan Ridder, and Vince Carter slowly disappeared from Jordan's vision. 'He has left me!' was her first thought. But then she remembered something. She had thought the very same thing about Stan when he had not returned for her. 'What would an Urumqi do...what would Oro do?' The pain in her leg caused her thought process to break. Fangs tore through muscle. The pain was blinding.

Chapter Six-
Of Elders and of Warriors

Yia stood unseen in front of the palace gates. She reached out with her thoughts. In one direction, she felt the slime and pollution of the wastelands. In the other, she perceived Tib's Temple, and the Urumqi within. 'Will the chest to me,' her thoughts whispered. At her side, the chest that had most recently rested within the walls of Tib's Temple now floated beside her in Imperial City, the heart of the Empire. 'Can the palace be breached?' Her thoughts echoed through the Qi. 'I shall try.'

A City dweller might describe the palace as a juggernaut of rock, a staunch entity of stone. But through the Qi, one can learn to see things differently. To Yia, the palace was a ripple in the current, an anomaly which other forces and currents sought to escape. A portion of its creation was said to be physical, but its binding and ostensible force stemmed from a much darker power. Maintained by the Emperors since the days of Olde, its power was linked to the man within. Yia reached out farther with her thoughts, sharpening her perception of the surface before her. Its network became visible. Parting the tiny grains of energy, she slipped unseen into the dark halls of Emperor Viron.

The inside of the palace was a perversion of life. As soon as one set foot in such a dark and evil place, an irrevocable change was bound to overcome any but the strongest willed. Distorted men paced the labyrinth of corridors; if they could even be identified as men. They scuffled along, deformed and hunched over. Some were products of the technicians' science experiments. Others were servants to the Emperor himself. For many, it had been decades since they had seen the sunlight. They passed close to Yia, some of them nearly grazing her skin.

There was no time within the palace. There was no day and night. There was no way for Yia to tell how long she had been wandering before she stumbled upon the throne room. She waved her fingers and her disguise slid away. Another movement of her wrinkled hand caused the metal door to melt away. Thick gray liquid sizzled on the rock that was the palace floor. "Kanoka, is it?" said Viron loudly from across the room. "I must admit, you're the only one of your pathetic gathering foolish enough to face me alone." He stood from his throne and sharply clicked his index finger against his thumb. The double bladed sword lifted itself from its resting place on the blank stone wall and moved neatly into Viron's hand.

"You were never one for words, now were you," said Yia condescendingly. A nod of her head slid the sword quickly out of Viron's hands, where it screeched against the stone floor. "Return him to me NOW," she growled. The very thought of being in such a dark and twisted place had caused Yia to momentarily lose touch with her sense of inner calm. Viron mentally regained control of his weapon. "Because there is nothing to discuss," he hissed with conviction. "Draw your weapon, old woman."

Yia silently removed her staff from the folds of her robe. The olive colored piece of wood was slightly curved, warped to a crescent from old age. Viron continued toward her. He held his weapon calmly at his side. As he stepped within striking range of the frail figure before him, he swung his arm inward. But Yia's staff was already there, mitigating the intensity of the Emperor's blow. "He should have never been your prisoner, let him GO!" hissed Yia, her sense of tranquility fading. Viron twisted his weapon away from Yia's and thrust his hand forward. Yia slid sloppily away from him, her staff bouncing noisily on the stone floor. "I have won," said Viron coolly. "And now...now it is time for you to die."

Mr. Marah indeed felt broken. Broken, not in the physical sense, but in the darkest part of his soul. For countless years, he had tried to put on the facade. He had tried to hide his weaknesses from his family. But now, all hope was lost. When it came down to it, he had chosen to walk away. With his foot and his will destroyed, he had walked away. But in his stream of consciousness, as he lay there in the mud, there was one thing that he did not understand. Before the Battle of the Temple, Vicky had told him the story of Oro Kanoka. Oro had abandoned the Urumqi because he had known what they were doing was wrong; as he lay there, this much he knew. But that had not been enough. Oro had confronted the Urumqi and set things right.

For all those years, the one thing that Mr. Marah had been sure of was his choice to run. But now he understood. One cannot run from fear or anger, for soon there will be nowhere to go. He should have faced the Guran then, and he swore not to make the same mistake twice. He let the Qi flow through him. His body rose from the earth. Although the wooden splint that had once carried his weight was no more, a certain power was keeping him from slipping to the ground. He set out at a quick pace back towards the battle. There was one last thing that needed to be done.

As the crimson mass of troops inched closer to the City's wall, the Main Man attempted to organize what was left of the Traditional force's right flank. "Warriors, form up in front of me; archers, get back up to the hills! We need you to take out..." "We can't, sir!" interrupted a thin man carrying a longbow. "Their archers are just over the ridge...we'll get shot down if we go back up there!" Those within earshot grew quiet. "Well...I don't know what to tell you," replied the Main Man. "I'm going to the front lines; if we die, we die as one," he shouted. Flanked by two Agents, he rushed towards his enemies, bashing in the skulls of those who dared confront him. He watched in horror as the Agent on his right cried out in pain. Dozens of troops littered the ground beneath him.

The boy with the backpack and the man with the hammer staggered up to the ragtag bunch of archers. "We can't do any good," stammered one of the archers. "If we go up there, we can't even fire a single shot before their arrows kill us!" The man looked up at the hillside. "Come with me," he said to the group. The boy suddenly looked away. "Thank you sir, but I must reach the front," he called. The man proceeded to scale the jagged hillside, followed by the group of archers. Peering over the uppermost ridge, he glanced down at the endless rows of troops. He then slid his hands across the cracks and fissures that squiggled their way down to the end of the West Road where the legions of troops stood idle. "Right…here," said the man suddenly. He swung his hammer far behind his back, and with a powerful blow, crashed the iron tool into the fragment of rock that lined the ridge. The piece of rock tumbled downward at a sharp angle, crashing against other crags and footholds, causing the entire half of the ridge to crash down upon the troops. "How…how…" sputtered the archers. "For a long time, they put me in a rock quarry. Now the tables have turned," said the man. "But who are you?' they persisted. "Kanoka…Steve Kanoka," he said.

"They've done it!" cried out the Main Man. He watched as the landslide collapsed upon the troops unlucky enough to still be standing in the gap. "We've got 'em! Now just hold the line," he shouted to the few remaining warriors. Two Mandos rushed forward; removing a roll of razor wire from his equipment pack, the first Mando grabbed the end of the line and tossed the roll to the other. They swept decisively across the blood stained rocks, cutting down those who tried to climb.

The boy with the backpack now sprinted dangerously close to the front lines, for he recognized a familiar face. Before the Empire's decree, he had attended the Carter school, and now he was face to face with Vince Carter's mother. "Dan," she said; her voice hinted excitement and confusion all at once. The two looked up towards the towers where the rest of the Urumqi elders were struggling to fight both the Elites and the wolves. "I think I can take out that tower," said Dan quietly. "What? Well try!" said Mrs. Carter, a tone of desperation in her voice. Dan unpacked a few capsules and proceeded to load the tube. "I need fire," he said. Mrs. Carter touched the wick with her staff and the fuse hissed to life. He raised the tube and aimed it at the outermost frontal leg of the left guard tower. Seconds later the tower collapsed, crashing down upon the upper ledge of the gate. Fiery timber knocked the closest group of Elites over the back of the wall.

"Go. Now!" shouted Mr. Ridder to the other Urumqi. The avalanche of rubble that had cascaded down from the wall as a result of the explosion formed a rough path to the top of the wall where Igni stood. Mr. Huila slid quickly to the front of the group. "You want him, or should I take this one…" he asked Ridder. "My pleasure," he growled back. "The rest of you ought to get the gate open…" With just a few leaps, he found himself atop the apex of the wall. "Kill them now!" screamed Igni. The remaining Elite warriors scrambled from their positions and inched toward Mr. Ridder. Without hesitating, Igni grabbed a crate, slid it through the flames, and hurled it toward his enemy. But the speed of an Urumqi cannot be matched. Mr. Ridder raised his hand; the box shot backward and exploded against an Elite, sending him toppling over the wall.

"Enough…we fight him together," hissed Igni. The group of Elites moved closer. Unbeknownst to the others, so did the Guran. He had hidden himself from view and crossed the front of the gate to the secret door from which he had entered the battlefield. Through an eerie spiral staircase he had floated to reach the top of the wall. He was just in time to see an Urumqi deliver a devastating blow to Igni. The Elite commander wavered precariously at the edge of the wall before falling to the dusty road below. The Guran's hand shot rigid and the Urumqi lurched toward him. "Tell me, are you afraid of dying?" cackled the Guran. Mr. Ridder could not breathe. The life was being choked out of him.

Mr. Marah had reached the wall. He looked on almost idly as Mr. Huila and the other Urumqi beat down the wolves and warriors that surrounded the gate wench. His eyes and his mind were focused on a different situation. He watched as the Guran tightened his hold on the throat of Mr. Ridder. 'Just let him die…the man hated you,' whispered the anger. But he did not give in. He took up Ridder's staff and struck the Guran with all his might. The end of the staff collided with the side of the Guran's head. Blackened blood oozed out from the place where the old man's head had once been. It sizzled when it touched the stone floor of the wall and then sublimed into a cloud of fumes.

Across the walkway, sparks shot from Mr. Huila's staff as he pried the giant metal hinge away from the stony wall. Igni looked up as he saw the massive metal plated gate falling down upon him. He squirmed away just in time; the gate crashed down beside him. "Storm the City!" shouted the Main Man from below as the metal plated gate tore itself away from its pivot. Aside from the groups of Agents and Mandos who were holding off the crimson troops, everyone in the valley scrambled forward, crushing the remaining Elites who scampered about the base of the wall.

Chapter Seven-
One Chance at Triumph

Young James Marah had no idea what to do. He had just witnessed Aaron Brown, the captain of the Mandos, being pulled by his feet through the drainage arc by an unknown enemy. He had heard the sounds of battle, and then silence. Max and Dave stood awkwardly behind him; he felt their presence, as if they were looking to him for direction. Aaron Brown had hunted the Marah family for nearly all of his life. He had accepted his role as a pawn of the Guran, carrying out the Empire's orders without a shred of empathy for those whose lives he shattered. But then something had happened. Oro Kanoka, an Urumqi, had shown the people of Uru how to care. He had spared the lives of many as to show the beauty of redemption. But James was not an Agent of the people; he was not a prophet; he did not preach the doctrines of peace.

Cautiously, he crawled through the drainage arc, motioning for Max and Dave to follow. Upon reaching the other side, he saw Aaron. However, what he saw was not Aaron, not in the sense of what young James had known. What he saw was a broken man, a man utterly defeated. His opponent stood over him. "And now," growled Qur'shan, "you must die." He swung the spiked ball high into the air. Many times, James had pictured a similar scenario, although in his mind, it had been him standing victorious over a broken Aaron Brown. As if crushed by an icy avalanche, he suddenly realized the foolishness of what he had been conditioned to believe. "No!" screamed James. He leaped forward, hammer in hand. Before the metal spikes could tear through Aaron's torso, he delivered a devastating blow to Qur'shan's side. Max and Dave stood silently in shock as

James delivered blow after blow, each time his hammer cracking against Qur'shan's heavy armor.

The final blow was to Qur'shan's head. Stunned by the barrage of hits, he could not stay his enemy's final strike. James allowed his weapon's handle to slide loosely through his hand. His fist now tightened just behind the hammerhead. He pulled his arm back, not in perfect form, but in the way that felt right. Unleashing a lifetime of frustration, he threw himself forward. The hammerhead collided dully with the steel helmet. It was the final blow.

Qur'shan knew he had lost the battle…but yet, that was not all he knew. He gazed upward, dreamily, at young James Marah who stood menacingly over him. He could not think. He could not understand what it was that he was supposed to do in this final moment. The man standing over him looked right at him. "You have Sabrina's eyes," he said desperately. The expression on James Marah's face shifted drastically from one of rage to one of utter astonishment. "What did you say?" He was trying hard not to sound afraid, but was failing miserably. "Are you her…her son?" wept Qur'shan, completely losing control. "How do you know my mother?" asked James more calmly this time. "I knew her…like a husband knows his wife…but then…she left…"

Aaron had recovered slightly, and attempted to crawl over to where the other two men were having their hushed conversation. "Sabrina…that was my real mother's name," he called out, just loud enough for the other two men to hear him. It was in that moment that it came to him. Aaron Brown finally understood what had happened just moments ago, and it saddened him deeper than anything he had ever known. "You're…you're my dad, aren't you?" said Aaron to Qur'shan. Both of them had lost their helmets in the battle; they looked upon each other for the first time as father and son. After a long moment of silence, Aaron mustered the courage to ask the question to which he had never known the real answer. "What happened?" he blurted suddenly. "Where were you when I was just a boy, when I was with the Brown family?"

Before Aaron could ask anything more Qur'shan cut in. "When...when your mom...before you were born...she left me when I joined the army...I don't know..." "And that's when she...uh...went with my dad then," said James, unsure of what else to say. Aaron's focus shifted to James. "Well...I guess that sort of makes you my brother," he said. Forsaking the Mando hand-to-heart gesture for a true handshake, he reached out his hand, and James helped him to his feet.

From the rooftop of the old building where Aaron's Mandos had once lived, Igni slinked along, flanked by several Elite warriors who had escaped the breach of the wall. "Heh, traitor!" he hissed, as he saw Aaron and James lift Qur'shan to his feet. "No filthy Mando's no good, his blood must be spilled," he cackled, and he leapt down from the rooftop, sword in hand. During the entire exchange, Max and Dave had stood silently, amazed by what they had heard. They were the only ones who saw Igni jump ferociously toward the three battle weary men. Knowing that he was not close enough to stop the death strike, Max Toko whipped a sword out of his scabbard and hurled it in Igni's direction. The blade struck Igni square in the face, forestalling him just enough to allow Dave to sprint forward with a devastating blow. Greenish looking blood oozed from Igni's helmet; the captain of the Elite had met his match.

"More of them, up there on the roof!" called out Max. Qur'shan, now standing, nudged Aaron slightly. "Son...what do ya say we give then one last 'urrah?" For the first time in a long while, Aaron smiled. "That's just what I was thinking," he growled. Before charging the group of warriors, he looked back at James. "Are you with me, brother?" James hesitated, but only slightly, only to realize that Oro Kanoka was right. "Let's do this," he said, and the five men sprinted toward the remaining Elites.

Oro could not begin to fathom how their delicate plan had worked in such a timely manner. Just as he reached the palace drawbridge, Aan and his group could be seen sprinting just ahead. He could see that Aan's party had only been slightly more successful than his own. With him came Wanda, Wendy, and Ja. Oro was surprised to see the small boy who he had learned, just hours ago, was Ja's 'son'.

However, they were not the only ones who stood at the palace entrance. The echo of Derek's footsteps could be heard as he walked briskly down the drawbridge. The seven Urumqi all drew their staffs. "Ah, look at you, standing there all courageous, thinking you're about to become heroes after the Empire falls at your hands," taunted Derek, never breaking stride. "It really is too bad that I happened to show up, isn't it? I suppose that all of you are planning to find a way inside so that you can confront the great Emperor himself." His pacing did not change. "And I also suppose that, based on your little rampage through the City, you intend on splitting up, thus leaving you with the choice of who must face me. And before you all jump to volunteer your lives to your precious Oro Kanoka, let me make it perfectly clear that I am more than capable of defeating all of you."

Derek was now less than five steps away from where Oro stood at the front of the group. With a wide sweep of his hand, all seven Urumqi flew backward. None of them had ever seen such raw power. "So who will it be?" taunted Derek. "Which of you is to die first?" Oro looked around quickly at the others. He watched as Ryan returned to his feet. Derek's taunting seemed not to be affecting him. "I once trusted you," stated Ryan calmly in a voice that the others had never heard. "Wanda and I..." he began, "we welcomed you into our circle even though we didn't know you." "And you betrayed us" said Wanda in almost a whisper. The two of them edged closer to Derek. "You made me look like a fool," stated Ryan, "and no one gets away with that!" He jabbed his staff forward and Derek fell over backwards. Oro couldn't help but notice the slight smile on Aan's face after hearing Ryan speak.

"Us five, we have to get inside!" called out Oro. As the group rushed up the drawbridge, Oro glanced back just in time to see Derek's weapon appear out of the nothingness. He was afraid that Ryan and Wanda might not be able to hold him off...but something was not right. Derek seemed to be ignoring him, focusing on his friends. 'He wants to kill them first...'

Yia no longer existed, at least not in the physical sense. She faded into the Qi, her mental presence momentarily escaping the palace walls and expanding out to encompass the entire West of Uru, stretching out as far as the Temple. 'Can you crack the palace?' came Yia's whisper in the circular room, where the ancient Mrs. Patal was also immersed in the Qi. 'I can try.' The response flitted back to the front bridge in the center of the City, where Oro stood perplexed. "This place..." said Vince. Silence. "Something is not right about this place...it stands, but it is not built..." Oro looked at him, not knowing what to make of the comments. "It is held tightly by the Qi," said Ja quietly. Oro now understood. Yia had told him that Tib had built the Temple using the Qi; she had said there was another place...another place equal and opposite. "Open your mind," said Oro to the others. "When you do so, the thing itself will disappear."

Inside the palace, Oro cried out in pain. His mind had allowed the parameters of the palace to vanish, but as he physically entered the void, his mind was entrapped. The many colored lights that he saw when he opened his mind in the daylight were now nonexistent. Instead, he felt like his brain had been dipped in a corrosive chemical. No matter how hard he tried to wipe it away, the source of the pain kept slipping away from his conscious thought. Blundering through the fog, he wracked his mind for the center, for the man he must defeat.

He did not know exactly how he had found it. He did not know how long it had been since he had breached the enchanted walls of the palace. He did not know why the pain had suddenly ceased. All he could think of was the crumpled figure that lay broken across the floor of the throne room. He ran toward Yia, temporarily forgetting that the others were looking to him for direction. "What happened?" he choked, kneeling beside her. She remained silent. She lifted her arm slightly, indicating the front of the rectangular chamber, where a man approached them.

There exists no way to describe the Emperor. To look upon him is to see the fear that wreathes in the deepest corners of every man's soul. His aura was that of blackness, blackness so deep that one might have trouble determining where his physical form began. The only contrast about him, the only thing visible through the blackness was his head. Unlike Derek, his hair was short, dark and knotted, as if it had been trapped beneath a warrior's helmet. His head was tilted downward, partially hiding his face, causing the front most curls of his tangled hair to slip menacingly forward. At first glance, his face appeared to be that of a young man, taut and shaven. But as he stepped slowly forward, and the torchlight shined upon him from a different angle, the deep creases could be seen, ghostlike, running across his visage.

He said nothing. He walked toward them. His steps were not as quick as Derek's had been, but twice as determined. Oro looked up to see a double bladed sword in the Emperor's hand. He knew that he had to think of something; he had to tell the others what to do. "Don't rush him," he shouted at the others. "We need to stick together!" The five Urumqi stood their line, determined not to give any ground. Ja edged up toward the left; Vince did the same on the right. "Keep to these flanks," hollered Aan. He looked over to Wendy. "Stay back," he told her, "I don't want you to get hurt." "But…" she tried to protest. "If one of us gets hurt, we will need you," he said with finality, pushing her aside. Oro glanced around at the others, starting with Ja and ending with Vince on the other side of the tight semicircle. To the latter, he gave a slight nod. "NOW," boomed Vince.

Chapter Eight-
One Final Moment

Vince was the first to strike. His smooth staff glowed, and he swung it powerfully toward Viron. As soon as his staff began to move, the iron sword was there to stop it. Vince cried out in surprise, almost dropping his staff due to the instantaneous deadlock that had caused his smooth weapon to reverberate awkwardly between his hands. The second strike came from Ja. With lightning speed, he jabbed his staff outward. The top of his staff grinded weakly against the middle section of the sword, which had somehow appeared right where he had planned to strike. Aan's strategy was somewhat different. While Vince relied on power and Ja on speed, Aan attempted to exploit the weakness of using a long, two-handed weapon by attacking head on. Gripping his staff tightly in his right hand, he rushed forward, moving his arm in an upward arc. As he had expected, his staff collided dully with the metal bar. Taking advantage of the momentary standstill, he thrust his left arm forward and grabbed hold of the sword's handle.

The moment the flesh of Aan's hand met the cold metal, the sword was wrenched away from him, and where the flattened middle section had just been, the sharp edge now swirled toward him. He hadn't even felt the blow. It was only after he saw the blood running down from the gash in his leg that he knew he had been wounded. He looked to Oro, and wondered why he had not yet attacked.

Oro did not know what to do. He had just witnessed a single man defend himself against a well planned attack by three Urumqi. Anything he might try, anything he might attempt to do, would surely be insignificant against the might of the

Emperor. Derek's words crept through him like poison. And then another caustic thought wrestled its way through his mind. He remembered what had happened in the mountains, what the bald man had said before Oro had vanquished him. Upon his death, he had uttered that the Urumqi and the Guranqi were the same. Somehow, Derek had known the very thing that Oro had just now understood. There was the Empire, or there was death.

He pushed forward. He could feel the Qi as it pulsated through his arms and shot forward toward Viron. And then, it was over. Oro saw the graying man flick his wrist. The four Urumqi were hurled into the air. When they fell, a sickening crack echoed throughout the room. Viron wasted no time. While the four attempted to recover from the crushing force that had knocked them downward, he reached out with his left hand, tearing a chunk of rock from the wall. It shattered into tiny, dagger-like pieces. Wendy did not have time enough to raise her staff. The rocks shot towards her, as if propelled by some unseen explosion. There was never a being as valiant as the little boy that Ja had raised. He tried to jump in front of her. But the daggers struck them both.

Oro found himself lying next to Yia on the stone floor. When he opened his eyes, he found her heaving, a thick yellow liquid pooled around her on the floor. He raised her head, he tried to help her. She was trying to tell him something, but he could not make out the words. "Not...me..." she coughed. "Go...HIM... ..." Her head fell limp in his lap. He did not understand what she meant. He turned his head to see Aan kneeling over Wendy. Ja had set down his staff to hold the boy. "May the stars watch over you," he whispered, and he told his son that everything would be alright. Vince had been hurled the farthest. At the back of the room, next to Viron's throne, he stood over an old wooden chest. With bare hands, he ripped away the lock and beheld the sapphire. He shouted out like a crazy man. "I have it!" he screamed. "We won!"

Viron turned to look at him. He pointed at the sapphire and it shattered in Vince's hands. The sharp pieces cut into Vince's flesh. He fell to his knees, as if the sole purpose for his existence had vanished before his eyes. Viron turned to face Oro. He opened his mouth to speak. For the first time, Oro could see the full length of his face. The aura that seemed to surround the Emperor swirled in his mouth when he spoke. "The people around you are dying," he said. "Leave now...and their lives will be...spared." Oro felt a cold pain radiate through the room; the sound of the word echoed through the room. 'Spared'.

Then all at once he understood. "She doesn't care if she dies!" shouted Oro. "Her dying wish is for me to destroy you!" Viron's eyes widened, but then instantly returned to normal. "But you...cannot do that. They...". Viron pointed at the other Urumqi. "...are smart men. They will take advantage of my...generous offer." Oro knew what had to be done. Once, long ago, the thing would have torn him apart, would have seemed impossible for him to ever accomplish. But the Battle of the Temple had taught him something. One person can have the power to change the course of history. One person can make others see reason.

"No, they won't!" screamed Oro. "Ja, think about your son! What kind of life will any other little boy have if you don't put an end to this tyranny? Wouldn't he want you to stop the evil that murdered his parents? Wouldn't he want...want the stars to watch over *you*?" The boy coughed; blood leaked from the corner of his mouth. He looked up at the man who had raised him and nodded. Ja stood beside Oro. "Aan!" boomed Ja. His voice had the power to make him tear his eyes away from Wendy. "You've had something that the rest of us never had," said Ja. "You've had someone who has stood by your side, even after your trickery led to the death of her best friend. Don't tell me you have forgotten Shelly," he said.

Aan stood and faced Viron, but his eyes wandered to Vince. Aan glanced at Oro, and then he too understood. "It's okay to be wrong sometimes," he said, looking Vince in the eye. "So the chest wasn't what we thought it was…that's okay. I've been wrong about a lot of things, but the one thing I was most wrong about was you. Just awhile back…" said Aan, "I thought you were a Guranqi. But now, I fight alongside you, to destroy that very same thing." At first, Oro could not tell what was happening. Vince began walking toward Viron; his face was expressionless. Viron still faced Oro; it was as if the Urumqi had been speaking a foreign language, for he seemed to derive no meaning from the words they had spoken. It was then that Vince chose to strike.

Chapter Nine-
And So It Was

The barrage of blows that assaulted Derek at the hands of Ryan and Wanda seemed to roll off of him like raindrops on a tilted glass surface. Most he deflected with his own weapon, and those that he did not seemed to sink into him, their power and momentum lost in a trap of darkness. Ryan jumped into the air and landed squarely behind Derek. A quick uppercut with the top of his staff sent Derek stumbling forward. "I don't know how much longer we can keep this up," whispered Ryan to Wanda. "As soon as we slip and let him take the offensive, we'll both be dead," she nodded back. Derek rolled back to his feet and sprinted towards them. Wanda's staff shone bright blue. She released a massive bolt of energy in Derek's direction.

Instantaneously dropping his double bladed sword, Derek raised both hands. A reddish glow, which seemed to pulse through his veins, appeared around the edges of his curled fingers. He forced the energy back toward Wanda, and he continued to sprint toward Ryan. The bluish mass crashed against Wanda; her weapon slipped from her hands as she was crushed against the cinderblock wall behind her. A flick of Derek's fingers pulled the sword back into his hands. The blow that hit Ryan was so powerful that he fell over backwards. His staff was locked with Derek's sword. He did not know how much longer his arms could hold. Derek slowly lifted his foot and kicked Ryan's arm. Ryan heard the cracking sound just before he felt the pain. His staff slipped out of his hands. Derek raised his sword. "Your life is now over," he said.

All Ryan could feel was the pain exploding outward from his broken arm. He opened his eyes. The razor sharp edge of

Derek's sword moved toward him; it felt like he was seeing in slow motion. The blade was a about foot away from his throat when he saw the staff enter into his window of vision. The sword collided with the staff and ceased to move toward his throat. He tilted his head slowly to the side in an attempt to see who had just saved his life. And that was when he saw Stan Mitchel. In a fury, Derek dropped his weapon once again and grabbed hold of Stan's staff. With all of his might, he tried to force the thin piece of wood from Stan's grasp.

Ryan looked up at the Urumqi who had just saved him. Stan's eyes flashed to the sword that lay at rest at Ryan's side, and Ryan knew what he had to do. Using the Qi, he lifted the weapon from the ground and thrust it into Derek. He saw the look of surprise in Derek's eyes; the cold white hands slackened their grip on Stan's staff. Derek was dead.

Vicky stumbled backwards, thinking about what the ghostlike form in front of her had said. 'You cannot destroy me with your hate.' It was almost impossible for her to consider…that within Kira dwelled a hate that dwarfed her own in comparison. The two continued to exchange blows. Vicky knew that, eventually, she would lose. There was only one thing left to try. She opened her mind, and she could not believe what she could now see. The presence that she felt in her wake was tortured, damaged, and nearly unrecognizable. Images of an old man beating a little, dark haired girl invaded Vicky's mind. An enlightened sense of understanding came over her. She blocked Kira's most recent blow and held her there, the sword locked into one of the jagged grooves that lined Vicky's staff.

"I'm sorry," said Vicky. Kira began to lessen the pressure she was placing against the staff. "I'm so, so, sorry," Vicky said again. Kira dropped her sword; Vicky let down her staff. "I understand what you've been through," said Vicky. "I've got a lot of bad memories that I'm not proud of too…but…but you can't let your hate get the best of you.

Just because someone's hurt you…it doesn't mean that everyone else wants to hurt you too." Kira stayed silent; her scowl had faded. "I have a…a friend," said Vicky, "whose gone to the palace to set right what he thinks is wrong in this world, even though there's almost no chance he'll survive."

Vicky paused. "I think I know why he went…he went because he understands that it isn't worth living a life that isn't your own. The Emperor sought to control him from the day he turned thirteen, so he's gone and done something about it." Somehow, saying the words aloud had caused Vicky to truly believe them. Kira smiled. "You are wise," she said earnestly. "Far wiser than my old master." She paused, as if to gather her thoughts. "This…friend of yours…he is a hero unlike any this land has ever seen." Vicky looked back at her. "I know." "I would like very much to meet him," Kira said. Vicky smiled. "I think you will have the chance, sometime," she said.

Nom saw the massive sword come crashing down toward him. There were several things that he could do. In mere seconds, he thought of the possibilities, many of them involving a quick parry with his staff, followed up by a devastating strike to the giant man's head. But Nom chose to play his strengths, to do what might ultimately end in the best possible scenario. He allowed the Qi to flow through him. He waved his arm forward and the sword stopped, as if blocked by an invisible shield. "Ahgh!" bellowed Gorath as he shifted all of his weight toward Nom. "What kind of trickery be this?" Gorath refused to believe that something he could not see was actually stronger than he was. "It is not trickery," stated Nom. "It is simply a reason."

Gorath did not understand what he had been told, so Nom kept explaining. "You see, when I asked you why you cared so deeply about the fate of the Empire, you could not provide me with an answer. I, however, have a perfectly good reason to be here. So, unlike you, my will serves me." Gorath backed away, almost frightened by what the little man in front of him had said. "If I were to kill you right now, you would be dying for nothing," continued Nom. "So join me, and I shall give you a reason to fight." A perplexed look shifted through Gorath's face. "And what reason be that?" he asked. "Only you can answer that question," whispered Nom. And so it was that Gorath understood.

Viron continued to face Oro, as if looking away might somehow cause him a great deal of pain. It was for this reason that the Emperor did not turn, did not see what Vince was about to do. The smooth staff glowed eerily in the darkening throne room. A streak of light flashed through the room as the weapon made its way toward its target. Viron screamed. The staff had collided with his shoulder. From where Oro and the others stood, the thin line of blood could be seen as it dripped from the narrow fissure in Viron's arm. "Even a Guranqi can bleed," said Vince.

The others wasted no time. Resuming their half circle formation, the Urumqi fought. Viron could no longer hold his own. He staggered back toward his throne, a look of desperation flitting across his face. Oro knew that it was almost time. He glanced at Aan, and nodded. The two Urumqi rushed forward, their staffs swinging inward toward the dark figure. Aan's blow hit first. The sword was forced from Viron's grasp. It touched the stone floor with a thud and continued to vibrate awkwardly. There was nothing left to stop Oro's swing. The gnarled end of his staff slammed against the Emperor's chest. He fell. Oro lunged forward, driving his weapon into Viron's heart. And then it was over.

Oro was the first to turn around. He saw Yia walking toward him, followed by Wendy and the little boy. None of them were bleeding; none of them looked ill. "His power is broken," said Yia before Oro could ask what had happened. They hugged. "But…this place…" started Vince, who seemed to be the only one thinking clearly, "if his power is broken, then shouldn't it fall?" "It will fall, once *all* of us depart," said Yia. She glanced toward the throne room entrance where a man slowly approached them. He looked utterly emaciated, yet a certain glow seemed to glint across his face. "Mom?" he said. Yia nodded, speechless. He stumbled toward her and they hugged. "Oh Todd, I thought I'd never see you again," sobbed Yia, trying hard to hold back the tears. When she saw Oro's confused look, she whispered to him, "Your father's younger brother."

Todd glanced quickly at the other people in the room. He focused on Ja, and could not help but feel something familiar. "Ja Kahn," he said. "Dad?" asked Ja quietly. Todd nodded his head. "No need to hide the truth now, Ja Kanoka."

Chapter Ten-
The Ships

It is at this point in my father's story that things started to become unclear. The last part of my father's story was told to me as he lay on his deathbed. Not all of the things that he said made sense to me, but I will relate them as best as I can. He said that after they left the palace, it fell. The people of the City rejoiced at the fall of their hated Emperor, and adopted the ways of democracy. The Main Man became the first elected leader of Uru, and he appointed the Big Man as his second in command. Steve Kanoka became the captain of commerce, and Gorath the captain of the safety force.

For the Urumqi, however, things were quite different. The elder generations chose to live in isolation, and the Patal house became their place of sanctuary. As for all of my father's friends, they chose to leave Uru forever. The ships had been restored to their full potential, and the Urumqi set sail in hopes of seeing the world. As for the reason, I am still not sure. My father never saw Caliphia again; he never had a chance to ask her what the bald man had meant. And Stan went on to tell the others of his adventures in the mountains, of the peoples he met. He talked of the beauty of those untouched by the Qi. Or maybe it was that my father had simply sought to understand the legend of Ben. The first Guranqi had come to Uru on ships, and perhaps he thought that there were more Guranqi to be stopped.

If my latter conjecture is correct, it would help to explain my father's final words to me. He said that after years of sailing, he came to another island. On this island lived the creator. My father confronted him, and asked him where the Guranqi had come from. "They come from me; I created them," he had said. "Then where do we come from?" my father asked. "Also from me. I wished to answer the eternal question of good and evil," the creator said. "Well you have your answer, good always prevails," my father said, "now we must destroy you." "Wait," said Aan. "If you kill him, the Urumqi will be gone forever. I will not let you do that." "As will the Guranqi be gone forever," said Kira. Kira had become an Urumqi after the fall of the Emperor. "You are right, I have been foolish," said Aan, "we must all fade."

And so it was that the creator was destroyed. The Urumqi lived in isolation on that island for a very long time. Upon old age, many built boats and sailed out into the unknown never to return. But my father stayed the longest. And it was here that I was born. When my parents died, I lived in solitude, and upon my old age, I too set sail from that island, only I found myself somewhere different. I had returned to Uru, and it is here that I write my father's legend so that the good people will never forget the tale of the Urumqi. My hand plagues me now from writing so much, but I do not regret it at all. Some warm water will feel good; I know, for my mother was a healer.

Index

Part One

1. Uru- An island, the known world
2. folk of Olde- the people who lived before or during the time of the Dreadful Day
3. Circle of Fire- the sun
4. Dreadful Day- the day that He came to Uru
5. West Hill- the highest of the hills along the West Road
6. The Great Circle- the buildings that made up the Temple are arranged in a circle. The courtyard in between these buildings is known as the Great Circle
7. Weapons- weapons were considered acceptable to be carried by anyone wishing to have protection, no matter what age

Part Two

1. West side school- the name given to Oro's school to distinguish it from the other schools set up by the Empire
2. East side school- the new Imperial school set up for those along the East Road
3. Imperial City- the only city in Uru, the home of Emperor Viron
4. Guran- literally the "ruler", he is the one who trains the young Guranqi adepts
5. the old oak tree- an ancient tree that overlooks the Crossroads in front of West side school

6. Crossroads- the place where the East Road and the West Road meet, right in front of West side school
7. Steve Kanoka- Oro Kanoka's father, son of Yia Kanoka
8. West Side Temple- the name that the Urumqi reinstate in place of "West side school"

Part Three

1. Battle of the Temple- the Urumqi way of referencing the fight at West Side Temple
2. Fell one- the Guran

Lyrics Cited

AFI. *Sing the Sorrow*. SKG Music, 2003.

Alter Bridge. *One Day Remains*. Wind-up Entertainment, Inc., 2004.

Creed. *Human Clay*. Wind-up Entertainment, Inc., 1999.

Simple Plan. *Welcome to My Life*. Lava Records, 2005.

Sum 41. *Chuck*. Island Records, 2004.

Scott Stapp. *The Great Divide*. Wind-up Entertainment, Inc., 2005.